Sienna

Annie Seaton

Pentecost Island 8

ANNIE SEATON

Dedication

This book is for all my loyal readers who wait patiently for the next book to be written

Thank you.

Acknowledgements

A special thank you to my wonderful editor and critique partner, Susanne Bellamy, and my eagle-eyed proof-reader, Roby Aiken.

Prologue

Odessa lifted her head and listened. She moved out of Dylan's arms when a boat motor broke the sweet silence that had surrounded them until a moment ago. She hadn't been on Pentecost Island long enough to be familiar with the comings and goings of vessels, but she had noticed a lot of small craft coming in from the yachts moored in the bay to visit the bar and restaurant on most days.

'Isn't it unusual for a boat to come this late at night? Pippa says it takes a very good skipper to navigate past the coral heads at the entrance of the bay even in the daytime,' she commented.

'It is late,' Dylan said quietly. 'I hope there's not a medical emergency on one of the boats. Not that there's a doctor here.'

Odessa stood beside Dylan in the quiet velvet darkness; he reached for her hand as they waited for the boat to appear and she smiled. He was a great guy, kind and gentle, and he knew when to be quiet and just enjoy living in the moment. She hadn't been romanced like this for a very long time—if ever— and she had a feeling the next six months on Pippa's island were going to be very enjoyable.

In the darkness, she was aware of Dylan lifting his other arm and pointing. 'Look, I can see it now. It's a tender.'

'I have no idea what a tender is.' Odessa heard the smart drawl in her tone, and she tried to bite the words back. Being snarky had always come naturally to her and it was one thing she was going to work on while she was here. It had become too much of a habit lately; she'd hidden behind that confident smart-mouthed front for too long. She cleared her throat. 'I'm sorry I didn't mean to sound rude. I assume it's some sort of boat.'

'I do love your posh way with words.' Dylan chuckled and put his arm around her shoulders. 'You *assume* correctly. It's a small rubber boat that sailors use to get from their yachts into the shore. Not for travelling across wide passages of water, although I can't see the lights of any boats out there tonight, and it's come into the bay.'

Odessa leaned back against him and closed her eyes again as Dylan's lips found their way to her neck. He lifted his head and she sighed with disappointment.

'Look, it's coming in near us,' he said. There was just enough new moon to see the silhouette of a small shovel-nosed boat speeding towards the shore. She held her breath, but the driver slowed before they reached the shore. As the vessel scraped on the shingly sand a person called out and jumped from the boat before running up the beach. The boat turned around and roared off into the night. Soon there was only the sound of the wash breaking on the beach as the motor faded into the distance.

'That was strange. I wonder where he's going now,' Dylan said. 'It makes you wonder if something illegal is going in. Although not the sort of thing I'd imagine would happen here with this island being so small and only a few staff, and not many guests.'

'I don't think it's anything like that. I'd swear that was Sienna who ran up the beach.'

'Come on, we'll go and check if it was her and make sure she's okay.' Dylan held Odessa's hand as they crossed the sand. Despite being almost midnight, the warm air caressed Odessa's skin as they walked towards the old house.

Oh, Pentecost Island is such a wonderful place. She was healing. Loved the island, loved the climate, loved the girls who ran it—despite her shaky introduction at Pippa and Rafe's wedding—and most of all, Odessa really loved spending time with Dylan, the resort's landscaper. She would draw the line at the 'L' word as to how she felt about him—she'd only been here a month—but if she was honest with herself, she already knew it was a relationship that was pretty special. The most special she'd ever experienced.

When they approached the small glade at the top of the beach path, the ragged sound of sobbing reached them, and then faded. They turned at each other as they caught a glimpse of a woman beneath the lights of the veranda of the old house as she ran towards the stairs

'It is Sienna,' Odessa said. 'I recognised her white jacket.'

'And her red hair,' Dylan said.

'I think this might need some girl talk.' Odessa stood on her toes and brushed her lips across Dylan's. 'You go back to your room, and I'll go and see what's wrong.'

'Try not to be too long. I'd like to talk some more tonight.'

She leaned in and kissed him again. 'Hmm, "talking" sounds tempting.'

'Okay, I'll see you soon.'

Odessa walked up the steps as Dylan headed around the side of the house to his room in the large shed at the back. The building of the new staff quarters up the hill had commenced and they, as well as some of the other staff, would each have a room there in a few weeks.

As she stepped through the front door, a light came on in the kitchen where Dylan had cooked her breakfast last weekend.

Odessa moved quietly through the living room and paused at the kitchen door. Her eyes widened and a gasp escaped her lips.

Sienna was sitting at the table, her head in her hands as she cried. Her white jacket was stained with blood.

Chapter 1

Pentecost Island - December

Sienna hadn't been back to Hamilton Island since she'd gone over for the girls' weekend with Evie and Tamsin a few months ago. They'd had such a good time over those three days, and she hadn't laughed so much in years. She hadn't had a lot to smile about before she'd come to the island, and forging new friendships with the women who worked there had lifted her spirits, She would be forever indebted to her best friend, Eliza, for suggesting her to Pippa for the day spa.

Sienna was very grateful to Pippa for giving her the chance to work on Pentecost Island, where the reputation of the "island of love" was quickly spreading. Pippa had giggled the other day when one of the guests had mentioned that—her boyfriend had proposed on their first night in one of the huts— and Pippa had immediately seized upon it and started work on an advertising slogan. Only married a short time, and with no honeymoon yet, Pippa was already back into her work, but Sienna firmly believed, it wasn't really work for her. For any of them really, it was such a good place to be. Whatever it was, Pippa, lived and breathed Ma Carmichael's Resort.

Everything about the island was fun, and the whole place seemed to run like clockwork with very little effort. Everyone who worked here seemed to love whatever their particular responsibility was. Nell and Tess in the office were always cheery, Tamsin, Cherry and Angus were always laughing in the kitchen, and when Eliza and Pippa held the planning meetings each week, there seemed to be more chat and joking than there was business discussed. Even Odessa had lightened up, and there was talk of her starting a small boutique next to the office down the track.

Sienna was determined to make *Hebe*, the day spa, a place where guests—both men and women—would come to Pentecost Island especially for the treatments, and then book a longer holiday. Her training in Switzerland had given her an edge on the treatments and products that were available up here in the tropics, although she had heard of an exclusive island further north that ran courses. Sienna was determined to upskill more while she was here, and make *Hebe* day spa even more exclusive.

So much had changed in the few months since that weekend away with the girls. Her best friend, Eliza, was settled with Phillipe—who Eliza said was the love of her life. Tamsin had met Gabe that weekend, and now they were a couple and expecting a baby. Evie's mysterious ex-husband had turned up on the island, and they had made up their differences and moved to the coast. Nell was with Nat, a guy from her past, and they were madly in love, and it appeared Odessa, the latest arrival to their island, had hooked up with Dylan, the gardener.

And now Pippa and Rafe were married. It was hard to keep up with the changes, and if Sienna was honest, she sometimes felt lonely when she saw all the couples together and happy.

As she sat at the back of Jiminy's boat on this fine Sunday morning in early summer, she wondered what on earth she was doing going over to Hamilton Island to meet Danny. Was it because she was lonely and just jumping at the first man who had smiled at her and shown her some attention? She needed to be very careful; she had seen what had happened to Eliza when she had been smitten with Rocco. Sienna had also seen the unhappiness of her mother when she had been let down by the man she thought had loved her.

Go carefully, she told herself. Do not trust.

She would never be taken in by a man like her father. Wonderful on the outside, but cruel and hard when he showed his true colours.

The weather this weekend was perfect; too good for the guests to be inside, and now that Pippa had bought six small catamarans for the guests to sail in the bay, the spa appointments had dropped when it was a fine day. Not that it bothered Sienna;

there was no way she could have kept that pace up without hiring another therapist. What bothered her was why she was jumping at Danny's suggestion that she come over for the day and spend it with him. Would she never learn?

Just for her day off, she told herself.

There was plenty she could be doing at the day spa, despite only having one appointment first thing this morning. She needed to practise the new treatment she had developed, her stock was running low and she should be back there placing an order, and—

She drew a deep breath as she stared out over the smooth silver Passage as Jiminy's launch took her to Hamilton Island—and to Danny Riccardo.

'Nothing fancy,' he'd said. 'We'll have a picnic at my favourite beach. You will love it, Sienna.'

Of course she'd agreed, even though she had been so disappointed with him at Pippa and Rafe's wedding. It still upset her when she thought about it. When she'd heard that Danny and Renzo had been invited to the wedding, Sienna had been excited. Over the weeks the Riccardo brothers had been working on the new buildings on Pentecost Island, Danny had taken every chance he could to come and talk to her. She had built foolish dreams in her head for the night of the wedding, but Danny had ignored her all night and she had been desperately disappointed. Since the wedding, he had been back to his normal attentive self, so Sienna had jumped at his suggestion, and organised for a boat ride to the island.

It had been like being back at high school when she'd had a crush on one of the older boys from the Catholic school beside the convent she attended in Lucerne before she'd been banished to boarding school. The same breathless anticipation, the same thudding of her heart that seemed to speed up whenever she saw him, and that wonder as she looked into his huge brown eyes, eyes that were framed by the longest eyelashes she'd ever seen. Danny was so good looking, yet he seemed totally unaware of his looks. The biggest shock, was that he seemed to like being with her.

With me, Sienna. She couldn't believe he was interested in her.

Trust. Go carefully, her inner voice warned her.

Yet, Sienna knew instinctively Danny was as interested in her as she was fascinated by him.

It had been like love at first sight for her and no matter how hard she tried, she couldn't put the feeling—or the temptation—aside. The instant their eyes had met outside the spa hut the first time he'd come to work on her building, her breath had been stolen away. Their eyes had met and held, and she could even imagine the music that would have played if it had been a scene from a movie.

Violins and flowers would have surrounded them.

A smile tugged at her lips as Hamilton Island—and the date with Danny—approached.

As much as Sienna tried to tell herself it was dangerous, and only because Danny was so handsome, she wasn't able to stop that breathless feeling that was building inside her now. There was no harm in flirting, she just had to remind herself. It was a game, and some pleasant company, and there was no future to dream about.

No future. She didn't want a future with a man.

She had to go back to Switzerland one day, and from what Danny had told her, he was on the islands to stay. Even though his Italian accent was strong, he'd told her that despite quite a few trips back to Italy, he'd grown up in North Queensland and he loved working on the islands.

Renzo was always interrupting them, with a sharp word and a glare at Danny.

'I don't think your brother likes me,' Sienna said one day when Danny was installing a new cupboard in the spa foyer. Whenever he was there working she would find a reason to stay. She could have gone back to the house while he worked, but she loitered, talking to him and refolding towels that didn't need refolding.

They *always* talked. After only three weeks, she felt as though she knew everything there was to know about Danny Riccardo, and she had been open with him. She had hidden her lack of self-confidence, and was sure he thought of her as a woman of the world.

'Ah, don't you worry your pretty little head about my big brother. He pretends to be angry at me, because he knows I like to have fun when I work. He'—Danny threw his arms into the air, and his black curls fell around his face—'he thinks work is serious, I tell him, Renzo, you are *too* serious. We must laugh and enjoy what we do. It is not all about chasing the dollars. He is not like the happy brother I looked up to when I grew up. He has turned into a businessman, and I do not like it.'

'What will you do?' Sienna asked. 'If you leave, I mean.' Her face fell, it wouldn't be the same here without Danny calling in and seeing her every day. Mostly with a smile, but occasionally with a flower he picked from the garden on the way over. She knew there were months of building work ahead for them here, and she really hoped he would stay until it was completed.

'Oh, I will not be leaving.' His beautiful eyes widened and his mouth tipped into a huge smile as he reassured her. 'I will teach him how to be happy again. Don't worry, I am not going anywhere. Why would I leave a job when I can look at a beautiful young woman all day?'

Sienna's face had heated and she'd looked away from those eyes. She knew it was all light-hearted flirting and meant nothing, She had to learn not to take Danny seriously, but it was hard when he came to the day spa at every opportunity.

And that was why she'd jumped at the opportunity to see him on her day off.

Her early morning appointment had been finished by nine-thirty, and that had given Sienna enough time to catch the morning boat back to Hamilton Island with Jiminy. Instead of her usual silk trousers and top, she had worn a pretty dress beneath her white jacket to the appointment, and had left the jacket on when she had boarded the launch in case the wind was cool. Jiminy had dropped off the housemaids who came over to clean the huts. She would be ready to catch the four o'clock launch back when he returned to collect them and she would do her inventory then, she told herself sternly.

I will!

Chapter 2

Jiminy raised his eyebrows as he eased the boat into the marina on the northern side of Hamilton Island. For a moment, Sienna thought it was because Danny was sitting on the wharf waiting for them, looking casual as he swung his legs nonchalantly over the side of the wharf. His attention seemed to be focused on the large batfish breaking the surface of the water near the pylons.

But Jiminy whistled and pointed to a huge superyacht moored at the end of the row. 'If I'm not mistaken, I'd say that's Zac Montgomery's boat.'

'Who's that?' Sienna asked, her heart quivering when Danny pushed himself to his feet and sauntered along the wharf towards them.

'One of the bad boy billionaires of Hamilton Island,' Jiminy said, shaking his head. 'If you ever meet him and he looks your way, you run a mile, Sienna. He's not a good person, but he can put on a very gentlemanly face. But when he arrives, it's a big cash injection into the island economy, so he's welcomed with open arms. He always has an entourage on his boat, and they're always big spenders.' He chuckled and waved to Danny. 'Pippa needs to get him and his entourage over to Pentecost. Have you got any flyers for the day spa with you?'

Sienna patted her tote bag. 'Always.'

'Leave me half a dozen and I'll make sure they get to the Montgomery boat.'

'Thank you.' She nodded and as she dug in her bag for a wad of brochures, Jiminy called out to Danny.

'Hey, Dan.'

'Jiminy, how goes it?'

'If I have to work on a Sunday, at least this is a decent job to have,' the skipper replied.

Sienna passed the advertising material to Jiminy, and Danny held out his hand for her to hold when she stepped off the boat onto the wharf. When their hands met, the usual zing ran up her arm and took her breath away. She fought for normality in her voice as she smiled at him. 'Good morning.'

'Want a lift back over at four, Sienna?' Jiminy asked.

Before she could reply, Danny interrupted. 'It's okay. I'll run Sienna back to Pentecost before dark. We have a picnic planned.'

'Okie doke. See you both on the island through the week.'

'Thank you for the lift over, Jiminy,' Sienna said softly before they left the pen to walk along the wharf. She looked down and realised Danny was still holding her hand. Smiling, she left hers there; it felt right. 'Where are we going?'

'I have prepared a special picnic lunch for you, and I have already taken the basket and the drink cooler to the most romantic spot on Hamilton Island. It awaits you.'

Sienna giggled. 'So with all the romantic couples and honeymooners here on the island, I guess it's going to be busy.'

Danny shook his head. 'No, I can promise it will be only you and me.'

'You have me intrigued.' She lowered her

lashes as his intense gaze snagged hers and a delicious shiver ran down her back. Her heart was just about jumping out of her chest, and her hands and legs felt shaky. She couldn't spend the rest of the day in this state. Maybe she shouldn't have come.

'It is nice to see you in a dress today.'

Sienna smoothed her hands nervously down the sides of her dress. 'I thought it would be cooler and I packed my swimming costume too.' As they walked into the sunshine, she reached for her floppy straw hat and put it on. The wind was brisk near the water and she kept one hand on top of it to stop it blowing off.

'Sienna?' They reached the entrance of the marina, and crowds were milling in the street ahead.

She lifted her head slowly and met his eyes. 'Yes.'

'I am sorry if I make you nervous. Tell me what I should do to make you relax with me. Is it because we are over here where there are many people?'

She hesitated before she replied. I'm sorry. I'm not very confident and I wondered why you wanted to spend the afternoon with me.'

'If only you knew how much I have been looking forward to today. It is all I have thought about all week.'

A flutter kicked in her chest and she looked up at him with a tentative smile.

'That's better,' he said.

Chapter 3

Excited anticipation of the day ahead kept the smile on Sienna's face. While they had walked through the busy shopping and restaurant area, Danny kept hold of her hand. They turned onto a narrow path off the crowded beach, stepping into the quiet and dim world of a lush green rainforest. Dappled shadows from the movement of the wind high in the trees created a lacy pattern on the path beneath their feet.

'Where are we going?' she asked as they left behind the happy noise from the beach.

Danny shook his head. 'You will see.'

'Just one clue?' she asked with a smile.

'It is a surprise.'

They continued through the forest and then came out beside the water again, and they stopped at rocks at the far end of the beach. To their left was a wide passage of water and another island. Unlike Hamilton Island, this island was high and mountainous and there were no buildings to be seen; she hadn't noticed it from the marina.

'Is there another resort on that island?' she asked to fill the silence.

Danny shook his head again as he let go of her hand. 'No, that's Whitsunday Island. It's a national park. I'd love to take you there one day, it's very beautiful.' His glance was hesitant. 'That is, if you would like to go there with me.'

'Maybe another day when neither of us are working,' Sienna said shyly.

'I think a day off seems to be a rare event for us both at the moment.' Danny gestured to the track. 'This way now.'

'I don't mind. I love my job.' Sienna followed him onto the path. 'It's not like going to work, living on the island and doing what I love. What about you?'

'Renzo wanted me to do a job on Hayman Island today, but I insisted on a day off.' Danny's accent was stronger as he spoke quickly. '*Si,* I do love my work, but it can be very hard working for your older brother. He thinks he can boss me around.' He stopped again as the track forked and reached for her hand. 'This way. One day I will have my own business, I think.'

'You've been busy at Pentecost Island since I've been there.'

'We have, and there is a lot more work to be done yet. You might get bored with seeing me there every day.'

'No, I won't.' Sienna looked at him curiously. 'So it's not the Riccardo Brothers business?'

'It is, but not me. My two older brothers, Renzo and Dante are the brothers in the business name. Dante has gone back to live in Italy to help look after our mother. I've only worked with Renzo for two years. I am the youngest in our family. That is why Renzo thinks he can tell me what to do.'

'It must be difficult.'

Danny's voice was tight. 'You don't know the half of it.' After a moment, he chuckled. 'And you don't want to, so let's not give a thought to work for the rest of the day that is left to us.'

'You have a strong accent considering you grew up in Australia.'

'My family—and my extended family up at Ingham in the cane fields, still speak mostly Italian at home so my accent stayed.'

'Just one more question.' She tipped her head to the side and looked at him as they strolled along. It was good hearing about his background. 'What sort of work did you do before you worked in your brothers' business?'

Danny looked to the left where another track led down to the beach; Sienna wondered if they were going to the small beach she could see through the trees or keeping to the forest path. 'This way, almost to our beach,' he said. 'Before I came here I travelled a lot and I did a bit of this, and a bit of that,' he said. 'A Jack of all trades, you could call it.'

Sienna didn't press him; she knew well what it was like to have secrets. Not one to talk about her past, she always preferred to keep it that way. Eliza knew some of her story but it wasn't one that

Sienna wanted to share—it was a past she wanted to forget— so if Danny preferred not to talk about his past that was fine with her.

'What about you? he asked.

'I'm very boring. Always the same as I do now.'

'Never boring.' Danny rubbed his thumb over the back of her hand. They walked along side by side and the only sound was the crackle of the leaves beneath their feet.

Sienna smiled. They could have been miles from anywhere; the forest surrounded them, but the track was well-defined and was obviously leading somewhere.

'Are you going to tell me about this beach we are going to?' she asked. 'You said "our beach."'

Danny's smile was sweet. 'All I will tell you is, it is somewhere beautiful. Even more beautiful than your island.'

'I can't wait to see it.' She didn't mind if it took a long time to get there. Walking along holding Danny's hand filled Sienna with a contentment she hadn't felt for a long time. She had worked hard in the day spa in the months she'd been on Pentecost Island, not giving herself any time to dwell on the past. Some nights when she sat on the veranda by herself, looking at the water, she wondered if she had done the right thing leaving Europe and following Eliza to Australia. It was a different world here, and at times, she was able to forget her life in Switzerland. Last year, the months when Eliza was missing had added to her constant worries. That, and her other experience, had left its mark, and although the scars were not obvious to a casual observer, Sienna knew they ran deep. Being relaxed with a man, as she was with Danny, was very much a change for her.

She took a deep breath and let it out in a sigh. Being on Pentecost Island meant no one had high expectations of her, and even though no one was checking to see that she was immaculately presented every minute of the day, old habits were hard to shake.

She had to remember that there was no one

here waiting to see her fail. No one waiting to criticise her every move.

That was why she loved being on the island with the girls. Pippa was the most incredible boss.

'All good?' Danny slowed his pace, and sounded worried. 'That was a big sigh. You are not sorry you came to see me today?'

'No, I was just thinking about the island, and how lucky I am. What a good boss I have. Pippa is amazing.'

'She is very organised and she knows exactly what she wants.'

'Eliza—we have been friends since school—wrote to me and told me about the island and how I should come and work here.'

'And you did.'

'I did, but I didn't expect it to be as good as she said it would be. She told me about this wonderful island where her life had been saved. I thought she was exaggerating.' Sienna bit her lip. She'd thought that Eliza had been overly impressed by Pentecost Island because of the dreadful life she'd had before she had escaped from her husband. Any new place would have been better than that life. Sienna would never forgive herself for not trying harder to talk Eliza out of marrying Rocco.

'You look very worried, Sienna. Don't be worried, we haven't got far to go. In one moment we will be back in civilisation. This is just a shortcut along the water to the bay beneath where I live. We can reach it by road but this is a much nicer way to come, especially from the marina through the forest.'

'Will I see your house?'

'No. You do not want to see that. Where we are going is much nicer. We will have a picnic lunch, and then we will swim and relax. Then we will have a wine to toast the sunset, and I shall take you back to your island in our boat.'

'Is that the boat that I have seen you come to work in?'

'No, that is the work boat with our tools and equipment. We—the family—have another boat that we use for pleasure.' His voice was eager, and

Sienna glanced sideways at Danny as he hesitated, and then spoke again. 'Are you happy to stay on the beach and then go back in the boat? Would you have preferred to go to a restaurant?'

'I'm happy with whatever you choose. I think it sounds very nice. It is good to be away from the crowds.' She swallowed nervously. 'As long as it is a big boat.'

'It is. Not as big as Jiminy's, but it is a decent size to cross the Passage.'

'That is good to know.' Sienna gestured to the water. 'It is big water for little boats. I am used to my calm lake at home.'

Danny chuckled. 'We're almost there. I'll set your mind at rest.'

Chapter 4

The light brightened as they approached the end of the path and ahead, framed by two huge mango trees, was a glimpse of sapphire blue water. In the middle of the vista a sleek white motor cruiser bobbed in the small waves. The lush canopy of leaves above thinned and sunlight lit the path.

'Almost to our beach. That is your taxi home, *bella*.'

Sienna wondered idly why Danny hadn't offered to come to the island to collect her, but she shrugged off the thought. As they got closer to the shore she drew in a short breath. 'Oh my goodness, I can see our island too. I didn't realise we were walking in that direction.' She turned to Danny. 'So your house is above here and you can see across the Passage to our island. I didn't think we could see Hamilton Island from our bay.'

'You can.' Danny stopped and put one hand on her shoulder and leaned down so that his cheek was close to hers. A citrus fragrance tickled her nostrils; she hadn't been this close to him before. Heat warmed her from her head to her toes as his smooth cheek pressed against hers. He lifted his arm and pointed across the water to Pentecost Island.

'Let your eyes follow where I am pointing to and keep your eye on the end of my finger as I move it downwards from the peak on your island.'

Sienna would have been happy to follow his finger for the whole day if it meant his cheek stayed against hers.

'If you look down the peak on this side, you should just be able to see a tree that is growing out of the cliff at a right angle. See it?' His warm breath puffed on her lips as he turned slightly towards her.

'I can.' Her voice was husky.

'Come down that ridge line and can you see the tulip tree with the red flowers in the top?'

Sienna shook her head. 'You are teasing me. You can't see flowers from this far away.'

'No, I am not. If you stare hard enough, you can just see a faint brush of orange.'

Sienna stood back and shook her head as she looked up at him. A little warm butterfly beat its wings in her lower belly as his lips tilted in a huge smile.

'You are so teasing me!' she exclaimed.

Danny's eyes crinkled at the corners and his perfect teeth flashed white as he stared at her.

***

Sienna held Danny's gaze and the strangest feeling ran through him; it was more than desire—although there was a lot of that surging through him too—it was more a strong need to get to know this beautiful woman, to make her smile and take away the shadows from beneath her eyes. To protect her and keep her safe, and make her happy.

He shook himself mentally and looked past Sienna. He'd never felt like this in all of his twenty-nine years, but there was no point in following that line of thought until he'd sorted out the mess in his life. He knew he shouldn't have invited Sienna over today, but when she'd told him she had a rare day off, he hadn't been able to resist.

Renzo had lost his temper—as usual—and demanded to know why Danny couldn't work when he'd told him to go over to Hayman Island.

Danny had stood his ground. 'Because it's Sunday. And I am entitled to time off as per the agreement.'

That had set fuel to his brother's temper. 'We do not work to agreements. We work when there is work to be done. How do we expect our customers to come back to us, when we say, "Ah, I cannot work it is a Sunday?" Pah!'

'Perhaps I want to go to church.' Danny had kept a straight face 'Our mama would like that.'

'*Non dire cazzate!*' Renzo put his hands on his hips and stared at him. 'All right, then. You can have one day off, but on one condition.'

'Oh?' Danny said, his temper about to match Renzo's 'And what would that be?'

'You do not go anywhere near Pentecost Island and that woman.'

Danny's tone was cold. 'And what woman would that be? Let me see, would it be Pippa, Eliza,

Nell, Tamsin, Cherry, Odessa or Sienna? Oh, not to forget Tess, the new receptionist, and of course there are the housemaids and the kitchen hands. Should I not talk to any of them?'

'Don't be smart mouthed with me, Daniel. You know exactly who I mean.' His brother's voice was like a whip. 'I've seen you over there, mooning over that little Swiss girl. You forget your situation.'

'Oh no, I will never forget the situation you and Dante put me in. And one I will be out of very soon.'

'You have made a commitment. Remember that.'

'How could I forget?' Bitterness laced his voice as he turned to leave the office at the back of his brother's house.

'As you are having a day off, perhaps you could take Lucia into Airlie Beach for lunch. A change would be good for her. Maria said she has been unhappy.'

Danny had slammed the door behind him.

His brother's suggestion did not deserve an answer.

'Danny?' Sienna's soft voice pulled him out of his thoughts. He looked down at pretty green eyes holding concern. 'Have I said something to upset you? You look angry.'

Regret flooded through him, and he opened his arms and pulled her close without giving himself time to think about what he was doing. 'Oh no, of course you haven't. I am so sorry. My mind was totally on something else.' As soon as Sienna rested her head on his shoulder, Danny knew he'd made a mistake.

A big mistake.

Her hair and skin held a beautiful fragrance, and he almost groaned as her hands tentatively slipped around his waist. They were standing in the path that led to the glade beneath his house, and he knew no one was there to see them, but he still felt guilty.

I should not feel guilty.

He had put Lucia and Maria on the ferry to the mainland an hour before Sienna had arrived, and they had decided to stay there for beauty treatments followed by dinner, planning to come back to Hamilton Island tomorrow. He'd had a horrible moment when Maria, his sister-in-law, had suggested that they should both go over to Pentecost Island and try *Hebe*, the new spa over there.

'I have heard very good things about it,' she'd said.

'Yes, it is very popular with the guests.' Danny had shaken his head in an effort to dissuade them. 'But the rooms are booked out for weeks, and we still have not finished the work over there. Wait a couple of months until the pool and the outdoor Jacuzzi are in. It will be a much better experience then.'

'That sounds as though it will be worth waiting for.' Maria smiled at him. 'We'll go to Airlie Beach for our pampering. Is that all right with you, Lucia?'

The short plump woman's dark eyes had glinted with malice as she'd stared at Danny and then she eventually nodded. '*Si.*'

All the pampering in the world would not make a difference to that sour face, he'd thought uncharitably. *If you hate me so much, just do what I want and leave.*

Danny would have liked to have taken the motor cruiser over to Pentecost Island to collect Sienna, but he hadn't been prepared to risk it. Renzo could be very hard when he was crossed, despite the fact that he owed Danny big time for the sacrifice he had made for the family.

His brother had a short memory when it suited him.

Taking Sienna back to the island after dark would be safe enough. Renzo would be out playing cards with his mates, and the women wouldn't be back until tomorrow.

Danny jumped as a lorikeet squawked in the tree above them. Sienna's arms stayed around his back and he rested his head on top of hers. 'I swore to myself that we would have a day together today, that we would talk and swim and share a meal, and watch the sunset but I promised myself I would not touch you. We have not even reached the beach, and yet here I am holding you in my arms. And I know that you belong there. I'm sorry, Sienna.'

She moved away and lifted her head, her green eyes holding his. 'Why be sorry? I am holding you too.'

Danny let go and brushed off her question. 'You are, and it is very nice, but I think we both need to have a swim. What do you think?'

'It is very warm, and I would love to swim. Are you sure there are no stingers or anything in here?' she asked with a frown. 'Pippa makes everyone wear stinger suits over on the island. I don't have one.'

'No, it is safe here. Even if it wasn't, the wind is blowing from the south. It is the northerly that brings the dangerous jellyfish to the islands.'

'How can it be safe here?' Her aristocratic nose wrinkled as she frowned.

'Renzo hired some contractors who have done an excellent job of putting net right across the entrance of our bay. It is so fine that no stingers can enter this protected bay.'

'We should do that at Pentecost Island. The guests tell me how much they hate having to wear those suits when they get in the water. I love to swim but I find it too confining in those suits.' Sienna's eyes were wide as she looked up at him and it was all Danny could do not to take her into his arms again.

'Pippa talked to us about that when she decided to put a pool in, and we explained that nets won't work there as the boats go into the wharf in your bay.'

Sienna pointed to their large white cruiser out beyond the buoys that held the net in place. 'But yours is there?'

'The nets are between the boat and the shore. We take a small tender out to get to the boat. It's kept in the boatshed over there.'

'Okay,' she said slowly. 'You have convinced me. A swim will be very welcome . . . and safe. I am getting used to all of the dangerous things in Australia.'

He turned to her. 'I hope you don't class me as one of those, Sienna.'

Her pretty lips tipped up in a smile, and he noticed how her eyes lit up when she smiled.

'No, I was talking about the snakes and spiders and the stingers, and the sharks and the crocodiles.'

He put his head back and laughed. 'Will it reassure you that I have lived in North Queensland for most of my life, and I'm yet to see any of them. In the wild, that is.'

Sienna put her hand on his arm, and her eyes were coquettish. Now she was flirting with him and he liked that.

'Now you are not being truthful with me. I've only been here a few weeks and I've even seen some spiders!' she said.

'I'm talking about real spiders. The man-eating size.'

'Man-eating?' Her eyes were dancing as she flirted with him and Danny ignored the warmth of her hand on his arm. 'Not woman-eating?'

'Yes, the ones you see on the documentaries, they are as big as dinner plates. *And* yes, they are man- and woman-eating! I have never seen one of them. But yes, I've seen plenty of your every day Incy Wincy spiders.'

Her laugh tinkled around him 'I have no idea what an Incy Wincy spider is, but I am guessing it is something very small like I have seen.'

Danny shook his head. 'You don't know your nursey rhymes. I have listened to my nephews and nieces recite that rhyme every time it rains.'

'Fair enough.' Her smile disappeared suddenly and her face closed. 'Where can I get changed into my swimming costume please?'

Chapter 5
Pippa

I balanced the small paring knife in my left hand and tried to hold the three mangos I'd just removed from the fridge in my right hand. The last mango was wet and slippery where juice had seeped from one overripe end and it began to slip from my fingers. As I closed the fridge door with my elbow, I juggled and balanced, but the three large pieces of tropical fruit hit the tiled floor, closely followed by the knife.

'Bloody heck,' I muttered beneath my breath and quickly moved my bare foot as the knife narrowly missed my toes and bounced off the tiled floor. This cooking caper had not been a good idea. I should have asked Cherry and Angus to cook a meal and bring it up.

As I bent to retrieve the fruit—two intact and one mango splattered over the white tiles—the screen door to the veranda opened.

'Blooming hell,' I yelled as I stepped into

the sticky mess.

'Hello, are you there, Pippa? Are you okay?'

'I'm in the kitchen. Come on in.'

I looked up as Eliza appeared in the kitchen doorway. 'You're early.'

'No, I'm not, we said eleven, didn't we?' Eliza's eyes widened. 'My God, Pippa! What are you doing?'

I turned and surveyed the usually clear granite worktops.

'You can barely see the gorgeous view out there today. My attention was immediately taken by that.' Eliza chuckled as she gestured to the mess on the counters and the floor.

'Rafe's coming home tonight and I decided to cook him a special welcome home dinner.'

'Hmm. I didn't think you cooked.'

'Hmm is right, and no, I don't very often. But so far I've made cold cucumber soup, even though it looks like mossy tank water. I did try to bake bread to go with it.' I pulled a face and gestured to the lump of glutinous dough on the sink, and then held up my finger wrapped in a Band Aid. 'This is from when I tried to butterfly a loin of pork to stuff with apricots. What a stupid thing to do, fancy trying to cut a slab of pork to look like a butterfly.'

Eliza began to laugh and I smiled with her. 'And that?' She pointed to the floor, where the mango juice was running along the grout between the tiles. 'I assume that is dessert.'

'Mango mousse. Rafe loves mangoes.' I shook my head and couldn't hold back my mirth. 'Stuff it. I think it's time for coffee.'

'How about I help you clean up the mess first, and then we'll have a coffee?'

'I won't say no to that.'

She laughed again as she reached down to pick up the mangoes I'd dropped. 'So what's for dinner?'

'I'll ditch the soup, take the pork down to Angus for him to fix it, and see if Cherry has time to whip up that mousse for me.' I shook my head. 'I should have known better. I hate cooking.'

'It's the thought that counts. I didn't realise Rafe was away. I haven't been off Phillipe's boat for a few days.'

'Relaxing?'

'No, working. I've been looking at ideas for the pool. Wait until you see what I've found.'

With Eliza loading the dishwasher, and me wiping the benchtops and washing the floor, it was not long before we were sitting out on the balcony with coffee. Eliza had brought cake up from the restaurant. 'Cherry wanted us to try it out. Salted caramel cake.'

'It's such a hard life, supervising a resort.' I sighed with pleasure as I took a bite and the moist cake melted in my mouth. 'Oh, yum. That is to die for.'

'So why the sudden domestic goddess cooking binge?' Eliza picked up her coffee and regarded me over the rim.

'Rafe's been in Brisbane at a book signing. He wanted me to go with him but I'm still hesitant about leaving the place. There's a few little bumps that we have to navigate and I like to keep an eye on things. And the staff.'

Eliza raised her eyebrows. 'Odessa?' She reached down to the satchel that she'd brought in.

'Yes, even though she's not staff, I still worry about her. She's had a tough time but I think she's starting to go okay.'

'You're a control freak, Pippa. We're all responsible for our own happiness.'

'I know, but if I can make things a bit easier for the girls, I will.'

'You always have done, or ever since I met you anyway.'

'Oh, you didn't know me in the "before-Pentecost-Island-Pippa days." I'm a lot more patient and settled than I used to be. Aunty Vi leaving me the island was a life changer for me.'

Eliza smiled. 'And so has having a fabulous man like Rafe in your life.'

'I sure can't deny that,' I said. 'I think Dylan's been good for Odessa too. She's mellowed.'

'He has. She is more settled. She was telling me about the silverwork she's doing.'

'Her work is really good. I was thinking about opening a boutique when we renovate the old house. What do you think about that?'

'What sort of boutique?' Eliza asked.

'Maybe beach stuff. Locally sourced and exclusive, like hand printed sarongs and the like, And of course The jewellery created on our island.'

'Sounds like another forward step to me.'

I chuckled. 'I still can't believe it's only been a few months off two years since I got the letter from the solicitor saying I'd been left an island, and here we are now talking about building more huts, putting in a pool and opening a boutique. The restaurant is up and running, and look how many staff we've got now.'

Eliza shook her head. 'I never thought it would take off so much when I offered to come in as partner. It's been an incredible success. I think you really picked where there was a need.'

I shook my head. 'You know, I think it was

more a fluke. Or being on the right place at the right time. It's our island that's half the attraction, it's such a beautiful place, and keeping it unspoiled and natural as an eco-resort, you wouldn't even know it was here. You could sail past and not even notice it.'

'I beg to disagree,' Eliza said. 'How many people were in the bar last Saturday night? I couldn't believe it. We might even have to extend the restaurant and bar to keep up with the demand.'

'No,' I said. 'I think we'll keep it small and intimate like we started out.'

'I agree, I was just sounding you out, but one thing I do think we need to do is put the prices up.'

'I was thinking that too. The higher the tariff and food prices, the more exclusive it is, and that drives demand. It also means we can have special deals, and not lose money.'

'By Gawd, woman, we're a great team,' Eliza said in a strong Cockney accent.

'We sure are, but one of the things that's

really attracting the girls' weekends is *Hebe*.' I watched Eliza carefully for her reaction. 'You know Sienna much better than I do. Do you think she'd be upset if I suggested getting a second therapist?'

'Normally I'd say she'd be fine, but I've been a bit worried about her over the past few weeks. She seems to have lost her spark.'

I leaned forward. 'I've noticed that too. I was worried she was working too hard; that's one of the reasons I thought about a second staff member there.'

'Any development on the Danny-Sienna romance front?'

I shook my head. 'Not that I've noticed. Although Sienna has gone over to Hamo for the day.'

'Maybe she's seeing him over there.'

'I doubt it. I think she was upset when he brought that woman to the wedding.'

'God, she was a sour cow. Phillipe and I sat with them for while and she spent most of the time glaring at any woman who came near the table.

Lucia, her name was.'

'I tried to talk to her too, but I don't think her English is very good.' I dug in my pocket and reached for a tissue and dabbed at my face. The air was heavy with humidity and a line of towering white clouds rose in plumes above the horizon. The wet season was coming.

'Still no reason to be rude.' Eliza clicked the mouse on her laptop. 'Nell emailed me the forward bookings this morning. The good news is, even with the construction work happening we are booked out until the end of March. I was going to suggest having an Easter special, but I don't think there's any need.'

'I agree.'

Eliza turned the screen towards me and looked like the cat that got the cream. 'One more thing before we look at the finances. Look what I found.'

I stood and walked around the table to stand behind her chair so I could see the screen without the light reflecting on it.

'Oh my God, they're perfect. I love them. Where can we buy them?' I leaned forward and looked closely at the day beds around the infinity pool in the image. At each corner of the pool and in the middle of the sides were tiled extensions that held day beds. Each bed had timber posts and privacy curtains.

'The good news is there is a supplier in Sydney. And I've called and the lead time is only two weeks.'

'Fantastic. I'll see Renzo and Danny tomorrow and get them to talk to the pool people.'

'They're doing a great job. And they are so fast.' Eliza scrolled down. 'I thought these tables would look good in the area adjacent to the pool too.'

'Nice. And yes. I'm so pleased we got onto the Riccardos.'

The mention of the builders made me think of Danny . . . and Sienna. 'Do you think Sienna's okay?' I asked. It still surprised me that with my unhappy background I ended up as mother hen for the girls on the island.

'I've been wondering too,' Eliza said.

'She just doesn't seem happy.'

'And she spends most of her time off in the day spa too.' Eliza frowned. 'I know she loves living on the island, and the work in *Hebe*. But if you think about it, the rest of us have partners, and she's alone.'

'Do you think we need to matchmake? Give Danny a bit of a push?'

'I know she's keen on him.' The smile spread on Eliza's face. 'I think that's an excellent idea. I think the problem is she's too shy. And I'd say Danny doesn't know she's interested. She can come across as very proper and aloof, but I know the fun loving person that's in there.'

'For someone as beautiful as she is, it surprises me how shy Sienna seems. She's always immaculately groomed and seems confident.'

'She does, but I don't think the confidence is there. I don't think she had a very happy childhood. I'm not breaking any confidence, because she's never talked about it, but I've always wondered.'

'Okay, that's our next task. Some careful and quiet matchmaking. Just you and me, I won't say anything to the others. Now, show me this spreadsheet, and then I'd better go down to the kitchen and see Angus and Cherry about Rafe's dinner.'

Chapter 6
Sienna

Not wanting to talk about nursey rhymes, or children, or getting into a discussion about why she didn't know the rhyme about the stupid small spider, Sienna waited for Danny to tell her where she could get changed.

He gestured to the path that led into the bush. 'If you follow that path, there is a small cabana at the base of the cliff. The door will be closed but it is not locked. It is private, and belongs to our family. My brothers built it before I moved here. You should also find some beach towels there.'

'Okay. I won't be long. Shall I get a towel for you too?' She turned and paused before she headed up the path. 'You are sure it will be private?'

He nodded. 'Yes, this is the only way to it. You can't get to it from the houses unless you come along the beach. No one will come along here, but in the small chance they do, I will ensure you are not disturbed. And yes please, to the towel.'

'I'll be quick.' Sienna put her head down and hurried along the path. As Danny had said, there was a small cabana there at the base of a rocky cliff. The small brightly coloured building took her straight back to her childhood holidays on *Lido di Venezia* when her parents had hired a beach hut on the long sandy beach.

Those were the days before *it* had happened, the days when they had been a happy family and she and Max had played on the sand.

Max was perfect. He *had been* perfect. All her memories of those three years were happy. Every one that was imprinted on her mind. Her parents had been happy, and her life had been normal up until that day.

How could one day change so many lives?

Sienna pushed the door open and closed down her thoughts. It was going to be a happy day, and she would not ruin it by thinking of the past.

She changed quickly into her white one-piece swimsuit, and quickly twirled her hair up and secured it with a clip from her bag. Slipping her green sarong over her arm, she put her clothes and her sandals into her bag before selecting two beach towels from the shelf.

Danny was standing watching the motor cruiser bobbing gently in the small waves breaking with a splash at the edge of the bay near the rocks. Sienna caught her breath. While she had been getting changed he had taken off his shirt, and now wore only a pair of white board shorts. Against the white fabric his tanned muscular legs looked even browner. He had the Mediterranean olive complexion. Letting her gaze run down the muscled and toned back, she finally forced herself to look away and put her bag down carefully on a rock. Her bare feet crunched in the shingly sand, and Danny swung around as she approached.

Heat filled her cheeks as his appreciative glance swept her from head to toe, and settled on the folds of the ruched white swimsuit she'd bought the weekend she was on Hamo with the girls. She'd fallen in love with it the instant she had seen it in the exclusive boutique. The neckline plunged to the waist, but modesty was provided for, by the small gold buttons that ran down the front.

His voice was husky. 'You look like a Grecian goddess, Sienna.'

The heat intensified as he kept looking at her. The swimsuit had been horrendously expensive, but the look on Danny's face made every dollar spent worthwhile.

'Thank you.' She grinned at him and ran towards the water. 'Last one in is a rotten egg.'

A wide grin spread across Danny's face and he took off after her as she ran for the water. They both reached the edge at exactly the same time and plunged into the warm water. Sienna swam out a few strokes and then dived down into the crystal clear depths. The sand was white and shards of sunlight rippled through the water. Small fish darted along the bottom and she held her breath as she struck out further. Eventually she had to come up for a breath and was surprised to see that Danny had kept up with her and was treading water only a metre from where she surfaced.

'The water feels wonderful,' she said as she floated beside him.

'It does. I try to swim here every night after we get home from work.'

'In the dark?' She frowned.

'Yes, under the stars. You should try it, it's incredible in the moonlight.'

'I am, what is the English word? A squib?'

'You mean you're not very adventurous?'

'I do.'

'Yes, that is the word, but I don't believe it.'

'I used to be brave when I swam in our lake. Sometimes when I was young, I used to swim until that first snow of the winter, but I grew up and became sensible, and lost my courage.'

Danny swam over to her, and shook his head and flicked his hair back. His brown eyes held hers, and despite the warm water, a shiver ran down Sienna's back. The old Danny who had flirted with her before the wedding was back.

'I think you are adventurous to leave home and move to an Australian island.'

Sienna moved her legs in a bicycle motion to stay afloat. 'I left home a very long time ago.'

'Tell me about you growing up.'

She shook her head. 'That is very boring. It was much more fun when I left boarding school and moved out. I travelled across Europe with Eliza between doing my beauty courses. Then I got a job in London, and we stayed friends while she did her carpentry course—'

'Her what?' Danny's eyes were wide. 'She is a carpenter?'

Sienna nodded. 'A very good one. Did you know she built the first few huts on the island, before Pippa hired you and your brother?'

'No, I didn't. I thought she was one of the owners and lived on her yacht with Phillipe.'

'She is and she does.' Sienna smiled as Danny shook his head again.

'No wonder she pays close attention to what

we are doing. I won't make such assumptions in future.'

'I'll race you out to the buoy,' Sienna called as she began to swim.

'A rotten egg race again?' Danny said as he took off a few strokes behind her. Sienna smiled smugly as she beat him by three metres. He didn't know that she had been a champion swimmer.

They frolicked and played in the water like children for an hour until hunger called. In between swimming, and diving, and watching the fish in the blue water, they talked and joked together.

As they waded through the shallows, Sienna pulled the clip from her hair and squeezed the water from her ponytail. She was relaxed in Danny's company and felt as though she had learned more about him in past hour than she had in the two months since she had met him. The only problem was, her attraction had deepened in that hour, and she now found it hard to look away from him. Not only that, she was also aware of his eyes on her.

He was such a good-looking man, and his

happy smile was hard to resist. She had laughed and smiled with him, until a fluid relaxation lightened her limbs so that she felt weightless in the water as she'd floated on her back beside him.

They walked up the beach together and, after Sienna had dried herself on the thick fluffy towel, she picked up her bag.

'I'll go and get dressed and make myself presentable.'

Danny's hand on her arm stopped her before she picked up her bag.

'There's no need to get dressed. Just put your sarong on and we'll sit under the trees and have some lunch. And then we'll have another swim later, so I can prove that I can win a race. I do not like being the rotten egg!'

'But—'

'But what?' Danny's arm slid around her waist, and the feel of his warm skin against hers chased away what she had been going to say. 'Um, I need—need to, I need to get tidy. I do not like looking— '

'Looking beautiful? Because you do.' His hands dropped away suddenly and he took a step back. 'Come over to the shade. I have a picnic that won't take long to serve. I'm starving.'

Sienna hesitated for a moment and bit her lip. Her hair was wet and in clumps, and her makeup had long gone, as she was sure the sun cream she had lathered on this morning had also. 'Okay, but I will just go and do my hair and put some more sunscreen on.' She turned and hurried up the path, aware of Danny's eyes on her back. Her legs were shaky and there was an exquisite longing tugging low in her belly. As well as combing her hair, and at least putting some lipstick on, Sienna needed some time away from him to regain her equilibrium. A couple of times when they were close to each other in the water, she had been tempted to lean across and put her lips on his, but had managed to resist.

Despite being wet and cool, she fanned her hand in front of her face as she walked to the cabana.

Pushing open the door, she put her bag down and looked in the small mirror that was above the wooden bench seat.

Her hair was sitting in damp strands, but her face had a pink glow and her eyes were bright and clear. Reaching for her comb, she tugged it through the dampness, and then twisted her hair back into a topknot and secured it with the clip.

Carefully she tied her sarong around her body, and then reached for her lipstick. She opened it and looked at herself again in the mirror. Her lips were a rosy red from the exertion, and she looked down at the pale pink lipstick. With a determined nod, she replaced the cap and slipped it back into her makeup purse.

It was because her lips were already rosy, Sienna told herself firmly and had nothing to do with the thought that Danny might kiss her.

Nothing at all.

Humming beneath her breath, she picked up her bag and headed back to the beach.

Chapter 7
Danny

Danny grabbed the beach towel and wrapped it around his waist before he walked over to the tree where he'd left the cooler. Their time in the water had passed quickly and he was surprised to hear the horn of the two o'clock ferry as it left the marina.

By the time Sienna walked down the path, he had unpacked the gourmet sandwiches he'd bought at his favourite coffee shop this morning, had two glasses topped with ice sitting on a tray, and had unscrewed the cap off the bottle of wine he'd packed.

He reached for his shirt as she spread her towel beside the log where he'd set out their lunch. 'It's hot. Don't worry about a shirt for my benefit,' she said softly. 'I'm still in my swimsuit.'

'Are you sure you won't think I have bad manners?' he asked passing her a bottle of water from the cooler.

'Thank you, and of course not. We're on the beach on a holiday island, and we'll pretend we are on holiday, not just having a Sunday off.' Sienna sat on the towel and tipped the bottle up. It was hard not to stare at the elegant line of her neck. Her skin was flawless, even without the usual makeup she wore.

Danny forced his eyes away and held up the wine bottle. He had vowed that he would simply spend the day in Sienna's company, and not give in to his desire. 'Would you like a wine with your lunch?'

'We are both European, so I don't think I need to think about my answer, do I?' she said playfully. 'Will you have one?'

'Just one glass, as I will be driving the boat later when I take you back.'

The silence was pleasant as they ate the sandwiches that Danny had packed and sipped their wine.

'Would you like some fruit for dessert, madame?' His eyes crinkled at the edges as she looked into the cooler.

'We have peaches and grapes. What would you like?'

'A peach please.'

He handed a plump pink peach over and as their fingers brushed they both pulled away, and looked down. Danny kept his eyes on the grapes as he picked them off one by one.

He cleared his throat. 'So how long do you think you'll stay on the island?'

Sienna shrugged. 'As long as I can stay working here with my visa. I love my job, and I am very invested in *Hebe*. It will be very hard to leave.' Her tone held mirth. 'Maybe I'll have to find myself a local husband so I can stay.'

Danny jumped up and knocked the wine bottle over. 'Don't even think about that. It would be a very foolish move.'

'I wasn't meaning you,' she said and her cheeks coloured in a blush. A trickle of peach juice ran down from her lips to her chin as she turned away, and the half-eaten peach rolled along the towel.

Danny reached for her hand, but she pulled away as he tried to apologise. 'That was very rude of me, please don't take it like that. I know you didn't mean that.' He leaned over and picked up a paper serviette. 'Sienna, look at me.'

She turned slowly, and her eyes met his. Tears hovered on her lashes. A shaft of longing hit him so strong, it made his chest ache.

He cleared his throat. 'You have some peach juice on your chin.' He lifted the serviette and Sienna stood stiffly as he dabbed gently. 'Really, I didn't mean to upset you. Honestly, It's just that I know someone who is in that situation and it's not a wise thing to do.'

'I was being flippant,' she said, as she allowed him to wipe her face. 'I am never getting married.'

'A sensible idea,' he said. 'What would you like to do now?'

Chapter 8
Pippa

I stood on the wharf as Rafe's black speed boat appeared as a small dot between Hamo and our island. The sun had almost reached the horizon with its usual Whitsunday blaze of glory. The heavy orb hovered in an apricot sky shot with slivers of purple and gold. A few months ago we would have all been down here toasting the sunset and our futures, but life seemed to have been too busy lately. That once dreamed of future of a functioning resort was now a reality. I made a mental note to book everyone for next Friday night for sunset drinks down on the rocks; it was a habit we had let slip. Christmas was only a few weeks away too, and we hadn't planned anything social yet. We had a great team on the island and even the new arrivals were fast becoming friends. A Christmas party was called for; I'd close the restaurant for one night and the staff could be rewarded for their hard work.

Tam and Nell were so settled on the island they had recently approached Rafe and I to buy a portion of land each so they could build their own homes. Nell had told me—on the quiet—that she knew Nat had bought an engagement ring for a Christmas engagement. 'He thinks it's a surprise,' she'd chuckled when I was in the office with her the day Rafe left. 'But the silly man used our joint Visa card, and I saw it on the statement. I can't wait to see it, Pippa, I am so happy.'

I was surprised when Nell's eyes filled with tears. 'So what's wrong?' I put my arm around her shoulder.

Nell shook her head and put her hand over her mouth. 'Nothing. I'm just so happy, it overwhelms me at times. I had no idea that my life would turn out like this when I agreed to come to Pentecost Island with you.'

'It's sure beaten my wildest expectations,' I agreed. 'Okay, so when's our next wedding?'

Nell grinned widely. 'I haven't been proposed to yet.' She pushed herself up from the desk chair and stood beside me. Her eyes filled with tears again as she held my shoulders. 'I'm so emotional these days and I hope he proposes soon, because I want to get married before June.'

'Oh?' I said. 'You don't want a winter wedding?'

Nell's grin was even wider as the first tear rolled down her cheek. 'No, I want to be married before I'm hugely pregnant.'

My high-pitched scream bounced off the walls as I grabbed Nell and danced around the room with her clinging to me. 'Oh my God, we're going to have two babies next year?'

'We are.'

'But only one wedding,' I said. As much as Gabe had tried to talk Tamsin into getting married before their baby was born in April, she stood firm. 'I don't have to have a piece of paper to make it formal. Our love is enough,' she'd told me.

'That's Tam and Gabe's call,' Nell said. 'I want to go the whole traditional route. The white wedding, the honeymoon, and a house.'

'And the good news I was holding in until Rafe was back, is that the subdivision of your blocks of land has been approved.'

This time Nell squealed.

'As long as you're sure you want to settle on the island,' I said wiping away my own happy tears.

'We are. All for one and one for all, remember.' Nell sat down and fanned herself with her hand.

'Are you well?' I asked. 'Have you been sick at all?'

'Yep, not like poor Tam. No morning sickness yet! Just tired and emotional.'

'When will you tell Tam?'

'Soon.'

Now, as I stood on the wharf watching Rafe come home to me, my happiness was complete. The three days he had been gone had dragged, and after years of sleeping alone I quickly discovered that I no longer enjoyed it. It was the first time we'd been apart since I'd moved up to his house.

Our house, he called it now.

Our house on *our* beautiful island.

His boat approached quickly and the white

foam kicked up by the inboard motors fanned out across the Passage. My husband of two months stood at the wheel, his jet black hair blowing in the wind. I lifted my phone and snapped a photo as he entered the bay. The black boat, the gorgeous man, the apricot sky and the silver water provided a perfect landscape shot. That was one to go on the wall in *our* house.

I reached down and threw the rope to Rafe as he cut the speed and the boat purred up to the wharf. He jumped out in one fluid movement, quickly tied off the rope and ran along to where I waited. I was in his arms and his lips were on mine within seconds.

Finally, after being thoroughly kissed, my husband lifted his head and smiled down at me with that intense blue-eyed stare I had missed. 'Next time I go away, you are coming with me, Pippa Rendell. No arguments allowed.'

I stood on my toes and brushed my lips against his. 'No argument given. I missed you so much. The days dragged.'

Rafe went back to the boat, collected his small suitcase and then linked his arm through mine as we walked up the steps to our home. 'I hope we don't have plans tonight, do we? I want you all to myself.'

I put on a sultry grin and fluttered my eyelashes. 'Oh, I do have plans for you.'

'You do?' His answering grin was wicked and I couldn't get up that hill fast enough.

'I do,' I teased. 'I've planned a special dinner for you, and then I have lots of news for you.'

'Good news?' His dark eyebrows lifted in a question.

'All excellent news.'

'I have an idea,' he said. 'Even though I'm starving, we'll have a late dinner. Why don't we jump in the spa and then rest for a while. You can tell me all the news then.' He slipped his hand beneath my T-shirt and his hand crept upwards.

A shiver ran down my back and my legs almost went to jelly. 'I think that's an excellent idea, but I don't think I want a rest. And the news can wait.'

We reached the top of the steps and Rafe put his suitcase down as he lifted my T-shirt over my head, and I started on the buttons of his business shirt.

'Excellent,' he said. 'We obviously have the same idea.' The last of the sunset was blotted out as his head lowered to mine.

Dinner was *very* late.

Chapter 9

Danny

Danny was pleased that Sienna had kept hold of his hand as they walked back into the restaurant precinct. They'd decided to have a coffee in town and then Sienna wanted to call in at the beauty spa beneath the hotel on Catseye Beach to check out their products. He couldn't believe how immaculate she looked after five minutes getting changed in the cabana after lunch.

But he was simply content to be in her company. The mood was happy as they had coffee and shared a piece of cake.

Then they had planned another swim, and would watch the sunset together before he took her back across the Passage.

'Do you have anything planned tonight when you get back to Pentecost Island?' he asked as they came out of the coffee shop.

'Not really. Why do you ask?'

'I was thinking about going to the store

while you checked out your opposition, and we could have a barbeque on the beach before I take you back.'

Sienna smiled and nodded. 'That would save me ferreting for something back at the house.'

'I wondered what you all did there. I thought you might eat in the restaurant every night.'

'Oh no, the food is too rich for me to eat there too often. And besides, since you and Renzo added those new huts, the restaurant is full each night. We—the staff—cook in the kitchen of the original house. Angus keeps the pantry and fridge stocked—meals are part of our salary package, thanks to Pippa—and most of us cook for ourselves. Sometimes we might take it in turns to cook for everyone and it's a good way to debrief after work. The best night is Monday when Cherry is off and she tries out her new creations on us.'

'Sounds like the perfect job.'

'It is,' she said as they reached the hotel.

'How long do you want to spend here?' Danny asked as they reached the hotel.

'Is an hour okay?'

'Perfect. It'll give me time to do some shopping. You eat steak?'

'I do.'

Once Sienna had entered the day spa, Danny called in at the general store, and when he'd shopped he took off up the hill behind the shops and headed for his house to collect some plates and barbeque tools. The last thing he wanted to do was take Sienna there.

He let himself in and put the shopping bag on the kitchen bench. Rolling his eyes, he tried to ignore the mess that surrounded him. The house was his brother Dante's house, and Danny had it rent free while his brother was in Italy. By the look of things—the health of their mother was not good—Dante would be away another year.

Until Lucia had arrived, Danny had kept the house neat and tidy, and had hired a cleaner once a week to do the floors and the bathroom. Despite the cleaner still coming once a week, the house was a pigsty. Lucia didn't put anything away, and when she cooked, she would go days without loading the dishwasher.

The one time he had raised it with her, her small black eyes had narrowed and she had shrugged. 'Not my job. You don't like, you fix.'

Danny pushed away the thought of her; he would not think of that problem today and let his bad mood ruin the perfect day with Sienna. Quickly loading a basket with plates, linen napkins, and the barbeque tools, he picked up the shopping bag holding the antipasto, meat and salad, and bread rolls, and then took the shortcut down the cliff to their beach. Quickly stowing the food in the cooler and snapping the lid back on, he turned to the path that would take him to the beach. With a frown he put a hand up to his eyes. The motor cruiser had been moved; it was now attached to the buoy at the southern end of the beach.

He stared for a while, but it appeared there was no one on board. If Renzo was on the boat and taking it out, Danny would have to get Sienna to the marina by four p.m. in time for her to catch a lift back to Pentecost Island with Jiminy.

Narrowing his eyes, he watched the cruiser, and pulled his phone out, hitting the speed dial for Renzo.

For a long while he didn't think it was going to pick up and then there was a click and a short, 'What?'

'I just wanted to check if you need me to get anything to take over to the island tomorrow.'

'No. I'm still working here. All good.' There were muffled voices in the background. Then Danny could have sworn he heard a giggle. A cold feeling consumed him; what if Lucia and Maria were over on Pentecost Island with Renzo? What if they'd changed their minds about where they were going?

'Are the girls over there with you?' he forced himself to ask.

'No, they're at Airlie Beach.'

Another muffled female voice in the background. Danny shrugged. It wasn't his concern who his brother talked to when he was working.

Maybe Pippa had gone up to the building site to talk to him before he knocked off. He knew Renzo would be back on Hamo by six to go to his regular Sunday night poker game at the club.

At least he knew the boat was his for the night. Maybe one of Renzo's sons had taken it out for a quick spin while he and Sienna had been in town. He knew two of them had come home for the weekend. 'Okay. I'll see you in the morning.' He disconnected and made his way back to the hotel to wait for Sienna.

***

Sienna was smiling and carried a handful of brochures when she walked out of the day spa and into the foyer of the five star hotel. Danny was waiting for her and her heart kicked up a beat or two.

'Worth the visit?' He smiled down at her and she enjoyed the surge of excitement that ran through her.

'Oh, yes. I made some great contacts and I've found this course I'd like to go to.' She held up the brochure with a tropical vista across the front. 'Pippa's been talking about getting a second therapist. I'm not supposed to know but I have my sources.' She smiled. 'If she does, it will free me up to extend my skills at courses like this. And there was a girl there who's looking for more work.'

'Good stuff.' Danny held out his arm and she slipped her hand through the crook of his elbow. 'Ready to go back to the beach now?'

'I am.'

It wasn't long before they were on the beach and heading back into the water for a swim.

'I might have a serious swim this time, if you don't mind,' Sienna said.

'A serious swim?' He raised his eyebrows.

'Exercise.'

'Sure. Go for it.'

'You get your exercise at work every day. You look like you work out at the gym too.'

'No, I don't, no time. But you go swim and I'll float around like a lazy log.' He trailed his fingers down her bare arm.

A sweet ripple of desire clutched at Sienna's stomach, and she lifted her eyes to meet Danny's. In his eyes she saw the instant he decided to kiss her and she couldn't help herself, leaning forward to meet him halfway.

His lips were soft and cool against hers, and she closed her eyes, allowing herself a few seconds of doing what she wanted to do. That was something that didn't happen very often.

Danny groaned and his arms went around her as they stood in the warm shallows, and the pressure of his lips increased. Sienna opened her mouth to welcome him and the world disappeared as he slowly slid his lips back and forth across hers. The noise of water lapping around them, the gentle wind and the cries of the birds all disappeared as warmth suffused her. Despite the warmth, goose bumps ran up and down her back and arms, and an exquisite pleasure tugged at her lower belly.

Finally Danny pulled back and rested his forehead on hers. 'I'm sorry. I took a liberty I promised myself I wouldn't take. But, Sienna, I cannot get you from my thoughts. I love being with you.'

She decided to be honest. 'I am the same, Danny. And don't worry, I won't read too much into a simple kiss that has celebrated this beautiful day we have spent together.' Pulling away from his hold, her voice was brisk, even though her insides and legs were jelly. 'Now I am going to have a swim, while you lie in the water like your lazy log.'

'I'll start to get the barbeque ready while you have your exercise. I'll enjoy watching you.'

Sienna walked into the deeper water and set off on a brisk swim. She hadn't wanted Danny to see she was upset, even though she'd told him the truth. She had enjoyed his kiss, but that didn't mean she was going to get involved with him, even though he didn't seem keen to get involved anyway. He gave off mixed signals, and she didn't want to get hurt.

She wouldn't get hurt. Sienna knew very well not to give her trust—or love—to anyone.

Remember Max, she told herself. Once she

reached the deeper water, she put her head down and focused her thoughts.

With each stroke, her mind yelled, 'Pull' as she relived the game that she had played with her little brother and the toy train he'd loved. To this day, she couldn't bear to see toys like that, and had avoided seeing her friends at home after they had children.

'Pull, 'enna, pull,' Max would squeal.

His baby laughter surrounded her as she churned through the water.

I loved him so much. His little voice churned through her head as she swam and she stroked harder and harder trying to clear the surging memories. Thoughts of dangerous creatures, sharks and stingers and crocodiles, were far from her mind. Now Danny was the only danger to her, and she had to do something about that.

Do something, do something, do something. The words blended together as she closed her eyes and swam harder and faster.

Sienna swam back and forth across the bay

until she was exhausted and could barely lift her arms. As she tried to wade to the beach, she knew she had pushed herself too hard, and as her legs gave way she sank into the water. Lying back in the warm shallows she let her fingers brush against the tidal ridges in the sand, and smiled as tiny fish nibbled at her toes.

But she knew she had found the strength to resist Danny. She was strong, and she would not be tempted and she would not be hurt.

She would not put herself in that place again.

***

Danny packed up the last of the dishes and leftovers and put them into the cooler bag, stowing the bag beneath the barbeque that he'd wheeled to the back of the cabana. On the way through the glade, he picked a frangipani flower. Sienna was standing near the edge of the water looking up at the stars, and he gently tucked it behind her ear.

'You are amazing,' he said looking down at his damp board shorts and crumpled T-shirt. He knew his hair would be a wild mass of tangled curls from the salt water.

'Amazing?' Her laugh was quiet. 'I don't think so.'

'You are, Sienna. We've been on the beach most of the day. We've been for a long walk, you've had a huge swim and sat on the sand and now look at you. You look like you've stepped from the pages of a beauty or fashion magazine. Your hair is perfect, your face is beautiful and your dress is unwrinkled. Your white jacket is spotless, and highlights your gorgeous hair.'

'I learned to be perfect at a very young age. But don't be fooled, Danny, it is only superficial. I am far from perfect within.'

He shook his head, and then was surprised by the bitterness in her voice; he hadn't heard that before. 'You are perfection.' Unable to help himself, despite his vow to himself that he would not touch her again, he held his arms open, and she stepped in and put her head on his shoulder. He lifted one hand and gently smoothed her hair. 'None of us are perfect. We all hide much of ourselves.' He lifted his head and looked down at her, her auburn hair glowing in the dim light of the new moon. 'Can we stay friends? Maybe until we can be more?'

Disappointment shot through him when she shook her head, but her words reassured him.

'Yes, we can stay friends, Danny, but we can never be more. If you knew the real me, trust me, you wouldn't want more.'

He spoke quietly. 'If you knew the real me, you would run a mile.'

Her head shook again, this time more vehemently. 'No, Danny. You are a good person, I know that, and I'm really sorry I have no more to offer you.'

His forehead rested against hers again, and he smoothed her hair with one hand. 'Don't say never. Let me get my life sorted and then be open to me. Will you agree to that?'

'I can't promise anything.' Tears filled her eyes as she looked up at him. 'But I have had one of the best days of my life today, and I love being with you. If I could be different I would agree, but I can't.'

'Why? Can you tell me?' His hands caressed her shoulders and for a few seconds she was tempted to give in and admit that she could fall in love with him.

'It is a long story, but all you need to know is what you see is not the real me. I strive for perfection in my appearance and in my manner, and in my work, to cover the person that I am. The person who is never good enough. The person who is lacking in everything.'

He shook his head. 'I can't accept that. I see you for what you are, Sienna. You are a good and kind person. A person I would find it very easy to love if I was able to.'

Sienna smiled though her tears. 'We are a fine pair, aren't we? Do you want to share with me what makes you so unhappy?'

'No, I can't. But I am hoping that very soon the source of my unhappiness and my dilemma will be gone. And then, I promise you, I am going to do everything I can to win your heart.'

'Oh, Danny, that is a beautiful thing to say, but please don't. There is no heart there to win.'

'I will not give up, I promise you that.'

Sienna knew her smile was sad. 'And I will not give in because it will only lead to heartbreak.'

Before she could step back, Danny pulled her closer, and she couldn't resist. She felt safe and happy when he was holding her. He ran his hands down the back of her jacket but she could feel the heat of his touch through the thin fabric. Sienna sighed, reached up and ran her fingers through his wild curls. It was as though her body had a mind of its own, but no matter how hard she tried, it was impossible to move away from him.

She felt safe.

And cared for.

Sienna leaned into Danny; her lips were a breath away from his. He lowered his head, and she opened to him, her hands running down his strong shoulders and slipping naturally beneath his shirt.

Danny groaned as she pressed her fingers into the warmth of his back. She welcomed his kiss as he deepened it, wanting, needing his mouth on hers.

'You are the most beautiful woman I have ever known,' he murmured against her mouth. 'You've bewitched me. You're in my blood.'

His voice was low and husky, and Sienna closed her eyes. A spark of mutual need passed between them as her heart pounded against his chest. She leaned against him for a moment and then lifted her head and smiled up at him as he lowered his mouth to hers again.

She was being very foolish, but her heart had taken over and was commanding her mind.

And her actions.

God help her, because she couldn't help herself.

Chapter 10
Sienna

Finally Danny lifted his head and stepped back. Sienna's chest was rising and falling, quickly, and she took a deep breath, unsure of what to say or do. Never in her life had she felt like that before. Being out of his arms filled her with a familiar emptiness.

Danny looked down at her as they both caught their breath. Sienna couldn't help smiling at him as he held her gaze. Finally he reached over and loosely linked his arms around her waist. 'It is good to see you happy, *bella*. It makes my heart sing that I can make you smile.'

'You make me feel. . . it is hard to find the right word,' she said softly. 'I guess it's because you make me feel good about myself. It's been a wonderful day. Thank you for bringing me to your beach. I will never forget today.'

Danny rested his forehead against hers and his breath was warm against her skin. 'Sometimes when I watch you when we are working, you look sad. When you smile, your expression lights up, but I do not see you smile very often. Tell me, is it because you would rather be at home in Lucerne? Are you homesick?'

She shook her head slowly, and lifted her head again. 'No. That is the last place I would want to be. It does not hold happy memories for me.'

'A broken heart? Or should I not ask?'

'Yes, a broken heart, but not from a man.'

'Would it help you to talk about it??

Tears welled in Sienna's eyes at the kindness in Danny's voice.

'I have never spoken of it. Not even to Eliza.'

His arms tightened around her. 'If it would help . . . '

'Let's sit on the sand for a while, And then you must take me home.'

The sand was still warm beneath their legs as they sat a little way from the water's edge. Danny sat behind her, his arms around her. Sienna leaned back and rested her head on his shoulder.

Taking another deep breath, she began to speak,

'When I was thirteen-years-old, my brother and I were swimming in the lake. He was only three, and he loved to be in the water. My mother was in her chair under the tree and watching him when I swam out into the lake. She checked on him and he was sitting up on the grass playing with his toy cars, and she read her book. She didn't see him run to the water. I think he was trying to come to me. When I swam back to the shore, he wasn't there. There had been no noise; he just went in over his head and drowned. Without a sound. We didn't find his little body for two days.' Her voice cracked.

'I'm sorry. That would have been unbearable for your family.' Danny's arms were comforting as they tightened around her.

'I've never told anyone about it, because I carried so much guilt. If I hadn't swum out—'

'Hush.' His lips were warm against her cheek, and she sighed.

'No, not yet. You will understand more about me, and why I will never marry. I want to tell you the rest. My father blamed me, and I could do nothing right from that day. I tried so hard to be perfect in everything I did, but my poor mama was in and out of hospital and my father, he sent me away to boarding school. That was where I met Eliza, and she was like a breath of fresh air to me. We had many holidays together, until the time came when I let her down too.'

Danny shook his head. 'You cannot blame yourself for things that happen. I am sure Eliza would agree.'

'I wasn't a good friend to her either. I should have tried harder to stop her making a mistake. A deadly mistake.'

Danny didn't ask what she was talking about. 'Sienna, I have only known you a short time, but I have seen how you are with people and I know you are a good person. That is very clear to me.'

'I try so hard, but I can never believe that I will make the right decisions. I shouldn't have accepted your invitation today, but I could not say no. I could not resist you. I am starting to care too much for you, and I will let you down too. I will not do that.'

Before she knew it, Danny's arms moved and she was lying against his chest. As she looked up at him, she could see that he was troubled and her heart sank.

'Sienna, you will not let me down, and I ask you to trust me. Trust me, until I can tell you my story. It is too soon, yet. There are others involved. Will you trust me?'

His dark eyes were intent on hers, and she nodded slowly.

'Yes, I will trust you.'

Danny's head lowered to hers, and this time his kiss held a promise as his lips took hers. She lifted her arms and put them around his neck, never wanting to leave him.

Eventually he pulled back and she caught her breath.

'I need to take you home before we both lose control, and cause too many problems for each other. I am not going to give up on you, Sienna. Can you accept that?'

She nodded, knowing that she couldn't bear to let him go. 'Yes,' she whispered.

'Just wait there and I'll get the tender out of the boatshed and take you over to the cruiser. It will only take us ten minutes to get to Pentecost Island once the motor warms up. It is very powerful and can go very fast.' Danny stood, pulled her to her feet, and kissed her again. 'We must go.' His voice was ragged. 'Or I cannot trust myself.'

'I trust you,' she said softly. Sienna crossed to the tree where the towels were spread and picked up her bag. She was very thankful they hadn't been lying here where it was more secluded when Danny had kissed her because she knew what could have easily happened.

She would not have been able to resist. Because Sienna knew she wanted Danny as much as he wanted her. The doors of the boatshed creaked open and then she heard a rough sliding noise followed by a splash as the tender hit the water. She hoped this vessel was bigger than the one on Evie's boat, because she wasn't sure about going out into the deep water in such a small boat.

Don't be silly, she told herself. It wasn't far to the buoys where the cruiser was moored; she'd swum almost to the buoys today. A motor started and then a light came on as Danny brought the small rubber boat up to the beach and jumped out.

'What about the towels under the tree?' she asked.

'I'll get them when I come back.'

'It's going to be a late night for you, and it's a work day tomorrow.'

'I'll be fine.' He held out his hand and helped her into the tender. 'Sit in the middle. No rogue waves will splash you there.'

Sienna did as he asked and sat straight and stiff on the wooden seat in the middle of the low boat, her bag clutched firmly in her lap. Danny climbed in and pushed the boat into the shallows with one foot, before starting the motor again and soon they were heading across the bay towards the large motor cruiser.

There was very little wind and even though the sea was like a mill pond Sienna's mouth was still dry with fear. She focused on her breathing and blocked her mind to the memories that tried to intrude. Memories she had summoned by being honest with Danny. She was fine when she was in the water and swimming but the thought of falling from a boat, and not having control had always frightened her.

He slowed the boat, turning it in a wide arc and then cut the engine when they were about fifty metres from the large boat. The small boat rocked in the wash as it crossed its own choppy wake.

'What's wrong?' she asked, clutching the side of the boat as panic clawed at her chest.

Danny's voice was low. 'I think someone might be squatting on the boat. I noticed it had been moved this afternoon, and now I'm sure I saw a light just go on and off in the cabin below decks.'

'What are you going to do?'

'I'm going to row the rest of the way, so they can't hear us approach, and then go onboard and check it out.' Danny reached over and gripped her hand, and his voice was low. 'I'll tie the tender to the back of the boat, but I want you to sit there quietly while I see if someone is there.'

Sienna nodded. She didn't think her legs would hold her anyway if she had to move. For the next five minutes the oars in the water were the only sound, and then a single bump as the tender hit the back of the boat.

'You stay here and keep quiet. I won't be long.'

'You be careful,' she whispered, her heart in her throat.

Danny tied the rope to the metal steps and went to swing himself up out of the boat. Sienna's hand went to her chest and she gasped as a sudden strong light flashed in their faces from the boat.

'You lying little shit,' a loud voice boomed from above them,

'Stay there, please Sienna,' Danny touched her shoulder briefly and pulled himself up the ladder.

'What are you doing here, Renzo?' His voice was like steel, and Sienna held her breath. 'You told me you were at work. Have you been on the boat all day?'

Renzo! It was Danny's brother. Sienna dropped her head into her hands. How guilty they must look skulking around and coming to the boat in the dark.

'What do you think you're doing?' Renzo's voice was slurred.

'I was going to use the cruiser to take a friend home, but it looks like you're otherwise occupied.' Sudden light bathed the whole deck of the large boat as another light came on and Sienna looked up to where the two brothers stood near the back of the boat. Renzo was bare-chested, and an unfamiliar blonde woman wearing only the bottom half of a bikini now stood on the top of the ladder peering down at Sienna. Her bare breasts jiggled as the boat rocked, and Sienna looked away, unsure of what was going on.

Renzo grabbed Danny's T-shirt and shook

him. 'I told you to stay away from that Swiss girl, but you can't keep it in your pants, can you?'

'Look who's talking.' Danny's voice was full of disgust as he pulled away from his brother. 'What would your wife say about you entertaining your lady friend on the family boat?'

'About the same thing that *your* wife would say to you, little brother.'

Sienna gasped and her world spun.

His wife? Danny was married?

Harsh words were flung back and forth above her, and Sienna couldn't believe it when the woman starting laughing.

'Bring your friend up here, Danny, and we'll all have a drink,' she said.

Sienna put her hands over her face. She had trusted Danny, and she had told him her deepest secret, and all the time he had been pretending to being interested, simply so she would sleep with him. She had not long ago told him she trusted him.

Disgust flooded though her and she felt dirty. Her father had been right.

All she wanted to do was run away from this awful, awful situation and hide, but she was trapped on a boat—a tiny boat—off an island. It was like something from a soap opera, but this was real.

Very real.

And she had no one to blame but herself.

Renzo's voice boomed again. 'Take the whore home and then go and wait for your wife.'

Danny charged at his brother, his fist raised and the woman screamed as the brothers' heads connected. Danny fell back against the side of the deck. Renzo lunged for him and threw a punch that connected with Danny's nose. Sienna widened her eyes as blood sprayed from his face. She felt so helpless sitting down here in this stupid little rubber boat, looking up at them.

If she knew how to start the motor, she would have untied the boat and headed to the shore. She looked down at the oars sitting on the floor of the rubber boat. As the idea came to her, she reached up to untie the boat and row to the shore. After all, she had swum that far today, and she knew how to row. Anger fuelled her.

As her fingers struggled with the knot the light from above was blocked as someone climbed down the ladder at the back of the boat. Sienna scurried back as far as she could without falling over the back of the boat, worried that Renzo had come to hurt her, after he had assaulted his brother.

'What are you doing? Quickly move to the middle again.'

Not that that was any better.

It was Danny.

Danny who had a wife. Sienna fought the urge to be sick.

Oh, would she never learn?

Chapter 11
Sienna

Sienna stared straight ahead as Danny clambered into the boat. He stepped past her without a word and started the motor. He turned the boat in a wide arc, away from the boat and away from the shore towards the open water.

'Where are you taking me?' Her voice was quiet and shaky.

'I'm taking you back to the island.'

He stood above her at the back of the small boat, one hand on the tiller as he steered them, and the other holding his face.

'Which island? Back to Hamilton? Drop me at the beach and I will walk back and get a hotel room.'

He leaned forward so she could hear him over the motor. 'No. I'm taking you to your island. It will take a little longer than on the cruiser, but the water is calm and still and it's safe.'

Sienna blinked as something wet landed on

her face. She looked down at her jacket and realised that the blood from Danny's nose had dripped onto her face and jacket.

Her fear about the trip across the wide waterway in this small boat was immediately replaced by concern. 'You're bleeding,' she said.

'I know.'

'You are not going to pass out and fall in the water, are you?'

'No, it's only a bleeding nose.'

It was hard to see in the dim light, but Sienna swivelled around looking for a rag or a towel to staunch the bleeding, but there was only a small bucket and a rope on the floor. Without hesitation, she shrugged her jacket off, rolled it into a wad, and passed it up to him.

'Thank you,' Danny's voice was muffled as he held it to his face.

She turned her back to him and squeezed her eyes closed as they crossed the open water. Goose bumps ran up and down her arms and she wasn't sure if it was the cool wind or her fear that was bringing them.

'Please, let us get there safely,' she muttered under her breath as she thought of all the dangers that came with being out on the open water in this tiny boat. They had no lights and any ships or boats that were travelling out here wouldn't see them. There could be whales or sharks or crocodiles, all bigger than the boat, that could roll them over in an instant.

Sienna let all those fearful thoughts crowd her mind because she didn't want to think about what Renzo had said on the cruiser.

How fitting, she thought. Her final mistake would lead to her death by drowning. A fitting punishment in a way, and she wondered how her parents would cope again.

'I will replace your jacket.'

She jumped as Danny spoke and then he reached over and put the stained jacket on the seat beside her.

'No.' The one word was curt.

'Sienna, please listen to me. I will explain

what you heard. What Renzo said.'

'No. Just answer one question. Do you have a wife?'

'I do, but—'

'But she doesn't understand you. I don't want to hear it.'

'No, that's—'

Sienna surprised herself as she raised her voice. 'I don't want to listen to you. I don't want to see you again, and I don't want to speak to you. You no longer exist in my world. Do you hear me?'

Danny stood straight and didn't speak again. It took twenty minutes before she could finally see the lights of Pentecost Island ahead. Danny slowed the boat to a crawl as they went across the top of the coral heads out from the jetty, and then he turned the tender to the island. A moment later, the aluminium base scraped onto the shingly sand and the tender came to a stop on the beach.

'Sienna—'

'No.' She picked up her jacket and then held her bag firmly with one hand and held the side of the boat with the other as she stepped over the low rubber side into the shallow water. She didn't care that her good leather sandals were in the water; she just wanted to get away from him.

'No. Just go. Leave me alone.'

'I want to make sure you are all right.'

'Just go.' Her voice was a screech, and she knew if she didn't get away quickly she would fall to her knees on the sand and cry. Putting the bloodstained jacket around her shoulders, she ran towards the path, pleased when she heard the motor start and the boat head back out across the bay.

Chapter 12

Sienna ran to the old house and was pleased it was in darkness. Through her tears, she could see no one was there. It was late, everyone would be in bed, ready for the start of the working week. Her legs were weak and shaking and about to give way, as she ran into the kitchen, flicking the light on before she sank into a chair at the table. Once she had composed herself, she would make a chamomile tea, and then go to bed.

And try not to think of the fool she had made of herself.

Composing herself proved impossible. Every time she managed to hold back a sob, Sienna thought of how Danny had kissed her this afternoon, and how she had been duped by a married man.

She was a stupid, stupid fool, and could do nothing right. Her father had told her that enough times, that she should have remembered. Being on the island with good people had lulled her into a false sense of confidence about herself and her decision making. Giving into the attraction she had felt since that first day she had seen Danny had been so stupid. She should have known after Pippa's wedding something was not right, but he could be so persuasive. She had listened and believed those sweet words he had fed her this afternoon.

I am a stupid fool.

The age-old story of a woman falling for good looks and a silver tongue. A ragged sob tore through her and as she put her head in her hands the screen door opened behind her.

'My God. Sienna, sweetheart, what on earth has happened? You're bleeding.'

She lifted her head and turned around. Odessa stood in the doorway, her eyes wide, one hand over her mouth. As Sienna shook her head, she hurried across to her.

Sienna managed to put one hand up and speak, but her voice was thick. Mortification flooded through her as she realised her nose was running. 'No. I'm all right. It's not me. Someone else was bleeding and they used my jacket. I'm all right,' she repeated dully. 'Please just leave me. I was about to go to bed.'

'No. I most certainly will not. You look terrible and you can barely speak.' Odessa pulled out a chair and sat beside her. 'Are you sure you're not hurt?'

'Oh, I'm hurt all right.' Sienna managed to pull a grim smile. 'Not physically, but my heart is hurting. Honestly, I'll be all right.' What she couldn't stop was the sob that followed her words.

The words that were at odds with her thoughts. Sienna knew she wasn't all right. She couldn't stay here. The thought of seeing Danny again—and she would have to see him every day while he worked on the island—filled her with shame. She would leave tomorrow. She would get Jiminy to take her to Hamilton Island and she would hide there in a hotel room until she could get a flight home.

Odessa crouched beside her and put one arm along her shoulders. 'I'm not leaving you while you are crying. I'm not going anywhere until I'm sure you really are all right. I'm going to make us both a hot drink. What would you like?' Odessa stood and walked over to the gas stove. On her way she took the box of tissues off the fridge and put it on the table beside Sienna.

'A chamomile tea please. The tea bags are in the cupboard next to the fridge. In the green box.' Sienna sniffed and reached over for a tissue. She dabbed at her eyes and then wiped her face. With surprise she looked at the tissue that was stained pink. 'I'm sorry. I must look a fright.'

'Love, you still look perfect after crying your eyes out. Now that you've wiped the blood off your face, you've reassured me. Now, reassure me some more, and tell me what the hell happened. Your jacket is beyond repair.' Odessa turned the gas on and set the kettle on the flame.

Sienna took a breath. What did it matter if she told the truth to Odessa? It couldn't make things any worse than they already were.

'Is the person who's bled all over your

jacket all right?'

Sienna shrugged. 'I think so.'

A few minutes later, Odessa poured the hot water onto the tea bags and came back to the table. She placed the mugs in the centre, and then when she was seated, she pulled the large mug across in front of Sienna. 'If you want to tell me what happened it will stay between you and me if that's what you'd prefer.'

'No, it's fine. I'll have to tell Pippa, and Eliza too.'

'Okay.'

Sienna sat straight. 'There was a fight and . . . and . . . Danny got punched in the nose and he had a nosebleed. I gave him my jacket to stop the bleeding. He was above me and some blood dropped down on me when he got back on the tender.'

'O . . . kay. Danny, as in Danny the builder here?'

'Yes.'

'So, is he okay? Was he assaulted?'

Sienna shook her head, and her hair fell forward. Her hands were shaking as she reached up to push it back. 'Not really. It was his brother who hit him.'

'Sounds like you've had a very dramatic night.' Odessa frowned as she reached for the other mug. 'Where did this all happen? Were you on one of the boats out past the bay?'

'On a boat, yes, but not here. We've been over on Hamilton Island all day,' Sienna said softly.

'My God!' Odessa's eyes widened. 'And you came all the way over the Passage on that tiny boat we saw? All the way from Hamo?'

Sienna nodded. 'Yes.'

'And Danny's gone back there now? With a bleeding head and an injury?'

'Yes.'

'I'm sorry, Sienna, but I think we need to call Pippa and Rafe right now. What if he passes out on the way back? It's not safe. Someone needs to make sure he gets back there safely.'

Weariness flowed through Sienna, but she

knew Odessa was right. No matter what Danny had done, someone needed to make sure he was safe. That's all she needed. Another drowning on her conscience.

'Yes, call Pippa. Ask her to come down and then I can tell her I am leaving the island tomorrow.' She managed to get the words out before she burst into a fresh round of tears.

Chapter 13

Pippa

It was just before midnight when I heard my mobile ringing inside the house. Rafe and I looked at each other over the candlelit table on the balcony; we had spent a most enjoyable evening making up for the three days he'd been away, and we'd just sat down to an extremely late dinner.

'Stay there,' he said as it stopped ringing. 'I'll get it for you. I pushed my plate away and frowned. A call at this time of night was never good news.

Rafe handed me the phone as he came back outside. 'A missed call from Odessa.'

As he sat beside me, I returned the call and it picked up straight away.

'Odessa, it's me, Pip. What's wrong?'

'We have a bit of a situation here. I think you and Rafe need to come down.'

'Guest problem?'

'No. It's Sienna. She's okay, but we need to talk to you. We're at the house.'

'Okay, we're on our way.'

Rafe and I quicky changed from our PJs and hurried down to Aunty Vi's house. No matter how long I had lived on the island, and how much the old house changed, it was still Aunty Vi's house to me.

The lights glowed yellow at the back of the house and we hurried along the veranda and into the kitchen. Odessa and Sienna were sitting at the table, both holding a mug. Rafe stood back and let me take the lead.

'Okay, so what's the drama?' I said as I stood there looking at Sienna. I didn't like to say anything, but she looked dreadful. 'Is that blood on your dress?' I looked at the jacket on the back of her chair and my eyes widened, as did Rafe's as he followed my gaze.

We listened and when Odessa got to the part about being concerned about Danny getting back safely, Rafe nodded and held his hand out for my phone.

'His number's in your contacts, isn't it?'

I nodded and handed the phone over. Rafe headed out to the veranda, and as I pulled out a chair and sat beside Sienna, I could hear him talking.

'So what happened? Why did Danny bring you home in a tender? It seems a really dangerous thing to do.'

Sienna shook her head slowly and when she looked up at me, her eyes were vacant. 'Neither of us were thinking straight. Renzo had the boat, and after he hit Danny I had to get home.' She looked up as Rafe came back in.

'He's home safe.'

Odessa and I both jumped up to grab Sienna as her eyes rolled back and she slumped in the chair.

'Rafe, quick, can you lift her down onto the floor. In the recovery position.' Since the resort had started up, every one of us had done our emergency first aid training. I looked at Odessa. 'Do you think she's taken something?'

Rafe laid Sienna carefully on the floor and

Odessa grabbed a wad of tea towels from the shelf, and put them beneath her head.

'No. I think she's had a shock. She's been coherent since I got here. Dylan and I were on the rocks and we saw her get out of the boat. She ran up here as though the hounds of hell were after her.'

Sienna's eyelids fluttered and she moaned softly and tried to sit up. 'What happened?'

I crouched down beside her. 'You fainted. Are you hurt anywhere?'

'No. I was just upset.'

We had a no drugs tolerance policy on the island, but I had to ask. 'Have you taken anything, Sienna?'

'No. I had a glass of wine this afternoon. Just one. I want to go and have a shower and go to bed.' Her voice was strained. 'I feel dirty.'

Rafe helped her to sit up and Odessa and I looked at each other. She gestured to the veranda and I nodded, before I followed her out.

She spoke softly. 'I only know what I told you about the fight and them coming back on the tender, but one thing Sienna did say was that she was leaving tomorrow. I think something's happened between her and Danny and she wants to get away.'

'Shit.' I shook my head. 'Sorry, that was unprofessional. You don't think he's assaulted her, do you?'

'No. I don't.' Odessa turned back to the kitchen. 'Do you want to talk to her now or in the morning?'

'Now, I think. I'll try and talk some sense into her. Where's she going to go?'

'Look, I'll just go and talk to Dylan. I'll stay in the house tonight and listen out for Sienna if you like.'

'Thank you, that'd be good. I appreciate it, Odessa.'

I stood outside the kitchen as she ran down the back steps and over to the building where she and Dylan each had a room. Although I did wonder if both the rooms were being used very often lately. Odessa and Dylan had struck up a close friendship.

I knew Rafe was pleased about it; he thought highly of our new landscape gardener.

I wondered how to handle this at this time of the night.

Eliza would be the one who would know what to do, and who could talk sense to Sienna. They had been friends since boarding school. I was reluctant to call her at this time of night, and I wasn't sure whether they were even moored at the island or had gone for a sail today.

Tomorrow morning would be soon enough, but I was not letting Sienna off the island until Eliza arrived. I turned to go back into the kitchen wondering how much to say.

Sienna was sitting at the table again and I was pleased to see there was some colour back in her cheeks. Rafe was sitting beside her and I took the chair on the other side.

When she spoke, her voice was stronger. 'Pippa, I am really, really sorry for all this. I want to explain to you what has happened and why I have to leave.'

Rafe met my gaze across the table and raised his eyebrows.

'I can't stay here with Danny working on the island every day, and I know he has to stay because there is still so much building to be done.'

I leaned forward. 'Sienna. If Danny has touched you, or hurt you in any way, he will not be working on the island anymore, so you don't have to worry.'

'Oh no, you can't do that. He's in enough trouble with his brother as it is. He didn't hurt me. I was stupid and trusting, and I just fell for the old lines.' She lifted her head and looked directly at me. 'I found out tonight that Danny has a wife.'

'Ah,' I said. 'Was that the short dark-haired woman with him at the wedding?'

'I guess it was. All I know is that he has a wife. Renzo abused him, and called him names before he punched him. Apparently *he* was on the boat with someone who was not *his* wife.' Sienna sighed and put her hand to her face. 'Danny asked him, "What would his *wife* say about him entertaining a lady on the family boat?" and then Renzo said, "About the same thing that *your* wife would say to you, little brother." And then they punched each other and there was blood everywhere.'

'You have had a big night,' I said.

'It's my own fault. I should never have gone out with Danny. If I had known he was married, I wouldn't have even spoken to him outside of work.'

'Are you sure it's right that he is married? It wasn't just Renzo talking?' I was trying to process everything my Riccardo builders had been up to. Talk about the lives of the rich and famous.

'Yes, he admitted to it when I asked him. I *have* to leave,' Sienna insisted. 'Immediately. I cannot stay with him working here every day. This island is too small. I would be very embarrassed with the mistake I made.'

I sat and looked at her for a long moment. 'No. You are *not* leaving. You have too much passion invested in *Hebe*, and we need you. I need you. You are one of us now, Sienna, and we look out for each other.' I stood and waited until she stood beside me. 'And don't blame yourself. You didn't make a mistake. Danny is the one who is in the wrong. He had no right chasing after you when he was married. Go to bed, and try to forget today. I will find a solution, I promise. Come up to the house when you wake in the morning, and we'll talk some more.'

Sienna's smile grew slowly, and I could tell she believed me. As soon as it was light I would ring Eliza.

And I would be talking to both the Riccardo brothers.

Chapter 14

Pippa

As it turned out, I didn't have to talk to the brothers; Sienna and Eliza came up with a solution, and then a call from Renzo Riccardo put the final touch on our plan. Sienna had called Eliza before I was even awake and I woke up to a text from Eliza, saying she and Phillipe would be in our bay by nine.

Rafe had gone down to talk to the Riccardos when they arrived at their usual time of eight a.m. and I waited with interest to see what information he came back with.

By ten a.m. he was still down there but the immediate problem was solved; there were smiles all around, even if Sienna's was a little bit fragile.

'Are you sure?' she asked for about the fifth time as we carried a pot of fresh brewed coffee out to the balcony. It was another brilliant day, and I knew that was making everyone seem a little happier.

'I am sure. It's called professional development, and with you already finding a replacement for while you are away'—I had already rung the therapist on Hamilton Island Sienna had spoken to yesterday—'you can leave as soon as you can get into the course.'

Eliza chipped in. 'We've already rung, and there was a place in the course that starts next Monday. We've booked her in. Now all we have to do is get her out to the island.'

Sienna had brought the brochures up with them, and I picked one up.

'Esculanta Island, north of Port Douglas. I've never heard of it, but wow, it looks like a fabulous island. There's a flight direct from Cairns.'

'Philippe and I moored there on the way here,' Eliza said. 'You have no idea of the level of luxury. It is supposed to be the only seven star island resort in the world.'

'Why have I never heard of it?' I said.

'Because they don't advertise. It has a different name on the map, and it's supposed to be a deserted island, but this resort was developed by a billionaire Englishman two years ago. It's a long way off the coast. It's where the international rich and famous go to be pampered.'

'When I saw the brochure yesterday, I had no idea it would be so expensive. Are you really sure, Pippa?' Sienna's eyes were wide but there were still shadows beneath her makeup.

'Yes. Eliza has offered to pay your way. I'll pay the wages for your replacement while you're gone.' I turned the brochure over and read the description aloud. 'The secluded island retreat is situated on idyllic sand-white beaches overlooking the dazzling blue waters of the Coral Sea. Bird of Paradise Spa has individual treatment villas. For couples, private suites are accessible via a secluded walkway over the water, allowing simultaneous treatments with spectacular views over the sea. The spa also offers vitality pools, steam rooms, saunas and Japanese water massage, with treatments inspired by age-old traditions that promote holistic rejuvenation.' I shook my head. 'I think we should have a girls' weekend in a few months.'

Eliza chuckled. 'We'd have to prise you

away from your husband.'

An idea took form in my head. Rafe and I still hadn't had a honeymoon. As though I had conjured him up by simply thinking about him, my husband opened the side gate and came out onto the balcony. He caught my eye and nodded slightly to me, and I knew everything had gone well.

'Coffee smells good,' he said rubbing his hands together. 'I'll grab a mug and then tell you all the good news.' My lovely man squeezed Sienna's shoulder as he walked past her on his way inside. 'You can stop worrying, Sienna. Danny's not coming back to the island.'

He was soon back with a mug, and the plate of salted caramel cake that we hadn't got to last night before the frantic call had come from Odessa.

'Renzo looked a bit worse for wear—he's got a good shiner—but he was very subdued,' Rafe said after his coffee was poured. 'He said Danny has gone away to work on another big project, and he has another builder coming here to take his place. Sienna, he particularly asked me to apologise to you for his behaviour last night, and to tell you he very much regrets that you had to witness the falling out with his brother.'

Sienna nodded and put her head down, but didn't speak.

'Sienna's going away for ten days to do a course later this week,' Eliza said.

'And then she's coming back to Pentecost Island to stay here,' I said with a smile.

An excellent solution all around,' Rafe said. He gestured to the cake on the table. 'Does anyone what to share the last piece with me?'

Sienna looked up and smiled. 'I think you deserve to have it all. Thank you, Rafe, and thank you, Pippa and Eliza for being so supportive. Her eyes were bright with tears. 'It's different for me. Apart from you, Eliza, I've never had support like this before. I've always had to stumble through and get myself out of trouble.'

Chapter 15
Danny

At six a.m. late on Thursday, Danny picked up his kitbag, and his laptop, and looked around the house he'd shared with Lucia for the past two and a half years. Although shared wasn't the right word for how they'd lived. He'd slept downstairs, and used the kitchen when she was next door at Renzo and Maria's house. When she was home he'd walked down to a café or a hotel and have a meal. Danny would never forgive his brothers for putting him in that situation.

A situation that had just stuffed up any chance of telling Sienna he was in love with her. He had no right to, and now, he knew he would never see her again. His heart ached as he thought about it, and he tried to hold back the anger with his family. There was nothing to be gained by blame.

The floor of the living room was littered with shopping bags; dirty plates and coffee cups covered every flat surface. But he could ignore the mess; he was out of here for good. The mess had nothing to do with the way he was feeling; the last few days had been the worst of his entire life.

Renzo had sacked him from the company, and then twenty-four hours later—after he'd sobered up and thought about the situation—had reinstated him. Danny had told him to shove it, and had found himself another building job up the coast within a day.

Maria, his brother's wife, had packed her bags and taken Aldo—the only child who still lived on Hamo with them—and moved north to her sister's farm near Ingham. Danny had heard the argument from next door, Renzo had grovelled, but Maria's screams had filled the air.

'Last time you promised it had only happened once, and I forgave you. How long has this one been going on, *tuo marito traditore?* I am going to my sister's and I will not be back. You will hear from my lawyer. *Sei un sacco di feccia.'*

Danny put his pillow over his head as the argument next door continued well into the night. He didn't blame Maria one bit. She had put up with

Renzo's infidelity for a long time, and he knew she'd forgiven him more than the one time she'd mentioned. She was right; his brother was a cheat and a scum bag. And the very reason that Danny swore he would never marry. Renzo's lack of commitment to his wife and family was a warning.

And Lucia . . . Danny shook his head; he couldn't stand to think about Lucia's intentions. A waste, a total bloody waste of almost three years.

And as for Sienna, his chest literally ached when he thought of never seeing her again. He now knew the meaning of heartbroken.

He pulled the door closed behind him for the last time. He would never come back to these islands; the memories were too sad.

##

The airport at Hamilton Island was crowded. School had ended for the year and locals were leaving the island to head to families around the country for Christmas. The December tourist influx had started and the noise and the bustle of the airport soothed Danny as he waited for his flight to

Cairns to be called.

When he'd walked in, he'd caught a flash of auburn hair in the crowd milling around the check in counter and he'd looked away. He didn't want that surge of longing to hit him every time he spotted a woman with the same colour hair as Sienna.

An announcement that the arrival time of the incoming flight had been delayed by a few minutes came over the PA system. Danny looked over at the café; the crowd had thinned and he decided he had time to grab a sandwich and a coffee before it was time for him to board. He hoisted his laptop bag onto his shoulder and walked across to the café.

Five minutes later as he sat at a high table and drank his coffee, the jet taxied to the tarmac outside the building.

His new life was about to begin.

No wife. No family. No women.

***

Sienna's stomach churned as she sat beside Eliza in the business lounge at Hamilton Island airport. The flight had been delayed slightly and Eliza had gone to the bar to get them both a glass of champagne.

'It might be early, but it will help settle your nerves a bit, love. And I don't have to drive. Philippe is waiting at the marina and we're going to have dinner on Hamo,' Eliza said as she placed two icy glasses on the table between them. She settled in the comfy sofa chair, and leaned back. Sienna met her gaze as Eliza's brow creased.

'For the tenth time today, Liza, I am fine. Stop worrying about me. I feel much better. Just embarrassed at the performance I put on.'

Eliza pulled a face. 'I know you too well. Your face is perfect, your clothes are immaculate. Not a line, not a frown, not a wrinkle on your face or a shadow under your eyes but I can tell when you're nervous.' She pointed to Sienna's foot as it jigged on the floor beneath the table. 'Aha! See!'

Sienna rolled her eyes, but she smiled. 'For the *eleventh* time, I am fine. Danny has gone from the island, and he won't be back. Yes, I'm upset, but you know me, I'm strong, I'll get over it.'

'You are strong.' Eliza raised her eyebrows. 'I hope I can believe you.'

'You can. I'm looking forward to this course and learning new techniques. And I'm super excited about seeing this resort. Seven stars! I didn't know they gave more than five.'

'I don't think they do.' Eliza's tone held cynicism and her gaze stayed on Sienna.

It was so hard to stay upbeat and pretend to be happy when all Sienna wanted to do was curl up in a corner. But she knew if she did that, Eliza would worry about her the whole time she was gone.

'But to be honest, we only walked past the pool to go to the bar when we called in there, and it was pretty incredible. The male staff were all in white tuxedos.' Eliza put her hand over her mouth as she stifled a giggle.

Sienna couldn't help smiling. 'What's so funny about that? I think it sounds very Gatsbyish.'

Eliza's giggle turned into a snort. 'Even the

pooper scooper men wore tuxedos and the shiniest black shoes I've ever seen.'

Sienna's giggle followed naturally. 'Pooper scooper men! What on earth are they?'

Eliza was shaking with laughter now. 'Oh my God. Wait until you see it. Behind the huge swimming pool, there's this spectacular water feature. A huge lake with an artificial waterfall cascading down a manmade cliff. It's really beautiful, but it has ducks paddling around on it, and what do ducks do?'

This time Sienna snorted as she remembered the trip she and Eliza had taken to Scotland when they'd finished school. They had spent the afternoon at a whisky distillery, watching the ducks in a pond in the garden as they floated around with their little bums sticking up in the air. She and Eliza had lost it; laughing until they cried. The more the other patrons looked at them, confused by what they were laughing at, the harder they'd laughed. The next morning they decided it was more the whisky than the ducks that had brought them undone. They each had the headache to prove it.

'Paddle with their heads down?'

Eliza snorted again. 'That too. God, I'd forgotten about that trip. We had the best time, didn't we? No, they poo and the resort at Esculanta Island have men in white tuxedos whose sole job is to scoop up the duck poo into little purpose-built poo collectors.'

'I can't wait to see it all. Maybe we'd better suggest that to Pippa for when the new pool goes in.'

'No, not that, but I do have some ideas for the pool.' Eliza's smile was wide. 'I am going to suggest we hire a pool boy who is built.'

'Built?'

'Built, as in a pleasure to look at. I want you to back me when I broach it to Pippa. You just check out the action around the pool at Esculanta. Phillipe almost had to drag me away. He reckoned I was salivating.' Eliza smiled. 'The pool boys wear the bottom half of a tuxedo only, and they come around with silver trays carrying hot towels to refresh the sunbakers. With silver tongs to hand them over.'

'No wonder Phillipe dragged you away. Okay, I'll check it out. This place sounds as good as it looked on the brochure.'

They both listened as the first call was made for the flight to board.

'Hurry up and drink your bubbles.' Eliza reached over and held Sienna's arm. 'Now despite your broken heart, I want you to promise me you'll try to forget you ever met Danny Riccardo, and have the best time while you're there.'

Sienna leaned forward and hugged Eliza. 'Thank you, *meine liebe Freundin.* You are the best friend a girl could ask for.'

Eliza hugged her back. 'And you remember that the rest of the girls on Pentecost care about you too. We're all worried about you.'

'All good. When I get back, I'll practise on you all. A pampering session.'

'Sounds good to me. Now have you got everything? Your bag? Your boarding pass?'

'Yes, Mama.'

They stood and quickly finished off their drinks, and headed out to the boarding gate. As she moved away from Eliza with a wave, Sienna looked up at the jet and she could have sworn it was Danny ducking his head to enter the front door of the plane.

She shook her head as she handed over her pass to the steward at the door. She was seeing him everywhere. That had to stop.

'Have a good trip, madam.'

'Thank you.' Sienna looked ahead as she strode towards the plane. That was the last time she would let herself think about Danny Riccardo.

Ever.

Chapter 16
Sienna- Esculanta Island

Being in the second row of the large jet, Sienna was first to disembark at Cairns airport. She glanced at her fine gold watch, conscious of the time; the slight delay on the departure on the flight from Hamilton Island made the time between the two flights a bit tight. At least she didn't have to worry about going to the baggage carousel to get her suitcase. She'd been assured as she'd boarded that her luggage would be sent across to the small airline who flew out to the island.

Excitement fizzed in her chest as she made her way to the lounge at the end of the building where her flight would board in fifteen minutes. The same as Hamilton Island, the airport was crowded with tourists in brightly-coloured clothes and looking relaxed and happy. For the first time since Sunday night, she let go of some of the sadness and tension that had held her in its unrelenting grip since Renzo and Danny had fought on the motor cruiser. She was going to do her best to put it aside and focus on this course. She had flown in early as she had decided to have a short luxury holiday for the weekend before she moved to the other side of the island where the course was being held. It was costing a fortune, but Sienna told herself she deserved it. Even though he had let her down in the worst possible way, telling Danny her story had been cathartic. This was the first step in her healing.

Somehow.

Pippa had smiled when Sienna had told her she was going to have a beauty treatment on the island while she was a guest. She had walked down to the wharf where Eliza and Phillipe had picked her up for the trip across to Hamilton Island.

'Sort of like a mystery shopper,' she'd said. 'You make sure you enjoy your time there, Sienna. You've been working very hard. Don't worry about *Hebe* while you're away. I was impressed with Jenny from Hamo when I spoke to her. Her light-hearted manner will entertain the guests, although I have a feeling she was putting it on a bit with all those jokes and funny sayings. She seems a bit of a character, but I did warm to her. She'll fit in well. If you're happy with her work, we might put her on as a second therapist and add another treatment room in the next couple of months.

At least Danny wouldn't be there to build it, Sienna thought.

Pippa's eyes had been kind and sympathetic as she'd looked at Sienna. 'That is if you've really decided to stay? You know we don't want to lose you? You're one of us now.'

'Yes, I've committed to you, and I love being on the island. And I love working with all of you. I've never had so many friends before. I'm here to stay for as long as I can.'

Sienna settled in a seat beside the window as she waited for her flight. Her phone buzzed with an incoming message when she turned it on.

Probably Eliza checking on her again.

Sienna's smile faded as she read the message from her father in Lucerne: ***Your mother*** *has been unwell but she is recovered now.*

The only messages she ever had from her father were sent with the sole intention of making her feel guilty, but she had long stopped letting them worry her.

Mostly anyway.

This message was having a swipe at her for being overseas.

Sienna's fingers flew over the phone as she sent a brief reply. ***I am pleased Mama has recovered.***

She was determined not to let the communication from her father bother her, and she focused on watching the planes take off and land. Gradually her breathing returned to normal and her hands relaxed in her lap. It was only a matter of minutes before a small plane with blue and gold writing on the side landed.

A *very* small seaplane.

Her excitement was replaced with nerves as she watched only four passengers duck their heads as they came out the low door of the plane. They were smiling and laughing, so the flight couldn't be that bad, she told herself firmly.

She'd had the choice between a fifteen minute flight or a two hour launch trip from Port Douglas, and the logistics of simply transferring flights was the easier option. It had been an easy choice, but now that she saw the tiny seaplane, her stomach plummeted.

The pilot exited the plane and walked across to the terminal; a tall man in a white shirt with gold epaulettes, he carried himself with a smile and confidence.

Maybe it wouldn't be so bad, she thought. It was a popular island, and no planes had crashed into the sea yet. When the flight was called, she stood, and then with a young couple, and another single woman, Sienna made her way to the desk at the door, her boarding pass in hand. The pilot was standing beside the steward at the gate and he smiled at each of them as they made their way to the gate.

'Good afternoon,' he said to Sienna with a

wide smile. 'It is a pleasure to have you on our flight, madam.'

She nodded and followed the three other passengers across the tarmac to the small seaplane. The pilot caught up with her as she reached the steps. He held the metal frame steady as the couple, followed by the other woman, and then Sienna climbed into the plane after them. She had to duck her head, and it was only the fact that the door closed behind her, and the steps were wheeled away, that kept her on the plane and hurriedly sitting in one of the six empty seats.

When she was seated, she realised that she'd sat next to the other woman who appeared to be travelling alone.

Once she was buckled into her seatbelt, her sweaty hands slipping on the clasp, Sienna leaned back and closed her eyes.

Fifteen minutes, that's all she had to endure, she thought, wishing she was back in her hut on Pentecost Island.

'You know the worst of these small planes?'

a shaky voice whispered beside her.

Sienna opened her eyes and for the first time took notice of the young woman she was sitting beside.

She shook her head. 'No, what is?'

'The fact that you can see through the windscreen in front of the pilot and watch him flying the plane. I swore I would never do this again after the last time.'

'The last time?' Sienna looked at the woman with the strong Irish accent who was probably close to her age.

'Yes, I was flying to a lodge in Canada in a plane just like this and when the pilot let go of the steering wheel, I screamed at him and asked what in the name of Mary and Joseph he thought he was doing.' The woman giggled. 'I really lost it. I asked him who was flying the effing plane.'

Sienna smiled, already enjoying her company. 'And what did he say?'

'He turned around and grinned at me, and waggled both his hands and said. "Mr Autopilot".

He asked me out for a drink when we landed, and I spent a few weeks in Alaska with him. And now here I am again. Another small plane flying itself. I should have taken the launch.' She held her hand out. 'Hi, I'm Isla.'

'I'm Sienna.' She shook Isla's hand. 'And I was just thinking the same thing.'

'Let's close our eyes and pretend we're on a bus,' Isla said, doing just that. 'We can talk with our eyes shut.' She giggled again. 'My five brothers tell me I can talk underwater too. If you get sick of me talking, just tell me to button it. I'm used to it.'

Sienna smiled again and put her head back and closed her eyes, but before she could reply, the microphone crackled and the pilot began the safety briefing. Once she knew where the life jacket was, and heard that they wouldn't be going high enough to need oxygen masks in event of an emergency, Sienna relaxed a little more.

As soon as their pilot stopped talking, Isla filled the silence. 'How long are you on the island for? You are obviously going for a holiday. You look very elegant.'

Sienna opened her eyes and looked down at her silk trousers and loose tunic top. 'This is pretty much what I wear all the time. Just in different colours. Easy to pack when I'm travelling.'

'Well, you look lovely. I always wear jeans and shorts, but I did pack a couple of dresses for the island. Are you German?' she asked. 'I'm trying to pick your accent.'

'Swiss,' Sienna replied. 'We speak Swiss German in Lucerne.'

'Lucerne! I was there last year,' Isla exclaimed. 'I had my photo taken on that gorgeous bridge with all the flower baskets.'

'The *Kapellbrücke?* The Chapel bridge.'

'Yes, that was it. Remind me to show you the photos on my phone when we land. I met up with this gorgeous Italian guy in Cologne and we travelled to Switzerland together in his old Kombi van. He was the best looking guy I've ever met.'

Sienna froze when Isla mentioned her Italian companion. That was the last thing she wanted to hear about.

Sienna's lack of response went unnoticed as Isla kept talking. 'I'm going over to the island to do a course there,' she said, opening her eyes again as the plane began to taxi down the tarmac. Isla shook her head. 'It still beats me how a plane can take off from a tarmac and then land on the bloody water.'

'What do you mean the water. I saw it was a seaplane but isn't there an airport on the island?'

'No, we come down in the harbour and then go into the marina. I read up my brochures.'

'Oh dear.' Sienna's mouth dried and she fanned herself with the boarding pass she was still clutching. 'I should have got the launch out instead of the plane.'

'I may still get it back, depending on how boyo here handles the water landing.' Isla gestured to the captain. She narrowed her eyes as Sienna watched her. 'Although he is quite cute, don't you think?

'Sssh. He'll hear you.'

'That's fine, lovey. Then he knows I'm

interested.'

Sienna couldn't help smiling. Isla was like a breath of fresh air. 'Okay, so tell me what sort of course you're going to do,' she asked. She wasn't sure if the beauty course was the only one, or if there was a training centre at the resort for different trades.

'Promise not to laugh?'

Sienna nodded, wondering what was coming.

'I mightn't look like one, but I'm a beauty therapist.' Isla's accent got broader the faster she spoke and Sienna had to concentrate to understand the words delivered in the Irish brogue.

'Excellent,' Sienna said. 'So am I. Doing the course too, that is.'

'Oh, how cool is that, darlin'! We can hang together. Although I must admit I did splurge. I'm having three days at the resort before the course starts. My dear Da sent me money for my birthday so he was sure I could eat for the next three months, but I figured I'd eat well enough at the resort to last me. Once I've tried out the cocktail bar and the restaurants, I want to check out the day spa.'

The giggle bubbled in Sienna's chest, and she couldn't help laughing as she held up her hand for a high five. 'Me too! The holiday for me as well and I'm planning the "mystery shopper" thing too.'

'Oh, that's even better.' Isla looked out the window and her eyes widened. 'Wow, look we've already taken off and we're over the water.'

'I have a feeling this is going to be a good weekend.' Sienna calmed and the ache in her heart lessened a tiny bit more. 'Now, Isla, tell me where are you from?'

By the time they landed with barely a splash, taxied across the water and disembarked, and were met by a welcome guide in the luxurious arrivals lounge, Sienna knew Isla's entire life history. Listening to her talk—and yes, it was true, she could talk underwater, but she was fun—had made the trip go in an instant. Before they knew it, the pilot was announcing they had arrived on

Esculanta Island.

The captain—who *was* very good looking—held Sienna's hand a little longer than he needed to as he helped her down the stairs. 'You are a very beautiful woman, *bella.*'

She stiffened when he called her *bella*, nodded briskly and pulled her hand away. Her heels clicked on the concrete as she crossed to the air conditioned arrivals room, and the welcome guide held the door open for her.

'Welcome to Esculanta Island, madame.'

Sienna smiled and waited for Isla to come in, but when she looked through the large window overlooking the marina, she could see her new friend, head to head with the captain. From a distance his dark hair and broad shoulders reminded her of Danny, and the ache in her chest came back with a vengeance.

Maybe she'd keep her distance from Isla; the last thing she wanted to do was spend time in a bar chatting to men who were on the prowl.

Yes, she nodded to herself. Quiet time alone,

to get ready for her course. That was what she needed and what she would do.

Sienna turned to the welcome guide and asked to be shown to her room.

Chapter 17
Danny - Port Douglas

Danny sat on the bed in the small bedroom at the Air BnB at Port Douglas checking his phone for messages. He had caught the bus from Cairns up to Port Douglas where the launch departed for Esculanta Island. Even though he knew Sienna was unlikely to contact him, he still held a slim hope. Pippa had his number and if Sienna wanted it, she could soon get it. He'd booked the room here for two nights because he didn't start in his new job until the day after tomorrow and then he was booked to go on the launch out to the island. Today was the day he'd set aside to talk to a lawyer, and get himself out of the complicated mess that his two brothers had got him into. Dante and Renzo owed him.

He'd made an appointment with a divorce lawyer in Port Douglas; he'd been grateful to get in at short notice. It was time to disassociate himself from Lucia once and for all.

God, he'd been so bloody naïve. And the promise of the money from his brothers had blinded him to the long term ramifications of what they'd wanted.

And the impact of what he had done by marrying a stranger—or a bloody fourth cousin ten times removed or whatever she was. All because Lucia Berretta had wanted to live in Australia, and his family owed her family from some feud decades back.

He had been the fall guy. The whole arrangement had been made before he'd even been asked.

No—not *asked*—before he'd been *told* what was happening and the telling had been sweetened with a significant cash deposit.

If he'd laid eyes on the sour woman before it was a done deal, he would have run for the hills. It didn't matter to Danny that she wasn't a particularly attractive woman; it was her sour face, her nasty attitude and her bitter tongue that he'd discovered after the town hall wedding in Castellina. And her absolute pleasure in making his life miserable when they were in the same place.

He'd never figured her out. Lucia had got what she wanted. Maybe it was genetic memory, the thought. A continuation of the family feud fifty years later.

Danny stared at his phone. No messages, no calls. He grabbed his clothes out of his bag and headed for the shower; it was almost time to leave for his ten o'clock appointment.

##

'It really is a difficult situation you are in, Mr Riccardo.' Mr James, the lawyer sat back and tapped his pencil on the desk. 'Even though I know as you say it was all organised for you by your family, you must take responsibility for going ahead with the wedding. You are the one who made the vows and signed the marriage certificate.'

Danny nodded. 'I know. And I very much regret that I agreed to the plan. Without going through all of the legalities one by one, can you just tell me the bottom line.'

'Very well.' The lawyer turned on his computer and didn't talk for a few moments as he read the screen and clicked the mouse.

'As you married in Italy, it potentially makes the situation even more problematic. The process can be long and expensive. Your wife—'

Danny shook his head. 'Please don't call her that. She has never been my wife.'

Mr James raised his eyebrows. 'Very well. This Italian woman has married you, an Australian citizen. I understand she would have applied for a temporary partner visa, once you travelled back to Australia.'

He stared at Danny as he nodded and held the lawyer's gaze steadily. 'This is where the sticking point is, and creates potential legal action for you. If you cannot prove a genuine relationship, and you are found guilty of arranging a marriage to obtain permanent residence for your spouse, the maximum penalty is a fine up to $210,000 and ten years imprisonment.'

Danny's jaw dropped, and his stomach

churned.

'What?'

'However, let us assume that the relationship was genuine and you are merely wanting to divorce.' He looked at Danny as though encouraging him to agree.

'Yes, let's go down that track. It was genuine at the time,' he said, swallowing the unpalatable lie. 'Lucia no longer wants to be married to me, or wants residency or citizenship'—he didn't repeat the harsh words she had thrown at him the other night—'she has decided to go back to Italy.' He looked at his watch. 'In fact she would be on the flight now.'

'Have you lived in Australia for the past twelve months?'

Danny nodded. 'I have.'

'Well, then, we can file for divorce without too much trouble.'

Danny's step was lighter as he headed along the beach at Port Douglas. A huge load had been lifted from him in that one simple meeting. Mr James had warned that the divorce would be a long process if Lucia did decide to contest it, but Danny couldn't see why she'd do that. One of the things she'd thrown at him was that she had a real man waiting for her back in Castellina. He had kept his cool and not demanded to know why she'd been here for the past two years trying to get citizenship, if that was the case.

After the formalities were completed, and the paperwork signed, he and Mr James had chatted about the tourist town and the local lawyer told him about the huge prawns that would come in on the trawlers late morning.

The older man looked at Danny. 'This is off the record now. I sense there is more that you're not telling me, but I've had an idea. Were either of you forced into the marriage under duress?

Danny's voice was bitter. 'I suppose you could call it duress, if I was told by my two older brothers that I was getting married to a woman I'd never met and that the ceremony was taking place the next day.'

'Excellent,' Mr James said.

'We've never shared a bed, if that helps.' Danny added.

'Non-consummation is an old law that no longer exists,' the lawyer said. 'However, I think we may have a solution. It's called declaration of nullity. Do you think your brothers would be willing to make an affidavit of what happened.'

'I'll make sure of it,' Danny said.

'In that case I'll apply to the Family Court on your behalf. However the bad news is it will cost you thirteen hundred and twenty dollars.'

'Mr James, that is the best news I've heard in a very long time.'

By way of a quiet celebration Danny collected two fresh bread rolls from the baker in the main street, a kilo of prawns, some seafood sauce in a small plastic container and a bottle of Coke and headed for the beach. He couldn't help thinking how it would have been perfect if Sienna had been beside him, but he quickly closed down that line of thought.

He would enjoy his own company for the next two days before he started his four week trial at Esculanta Island. If the work suited him, he would stay there for the six months contract they'd offered him.

And then he would decide where to go.

All he knew was he was not going back to Pentecost Island to work with his lowlife brother. His family no longer existed for him. He hadn't even told them where he was going.

Chapter 18
Sienna

A mix of hunger and curiosity chased Sienna from her room a few hours after she'd arrived. She'd unpacked and pressed all of her clothes with the travel iron she carried—she'd never trusted the irons in hotel rooms with her silk garments—and hung her clothes in the huge wardrobe. Her room was huge and looked over the pool to the sea beyond. The view through the entire glass wall at the end of the living room was framed by lush palm trees, and the best thing was the three rung stainless steel ladder that led from her balcony straight into the hexagonal swimming pool. Once she'd unpacked, she had slipped on her costume and gone for a quick swim.

Quick for her, anyway, as she did twenty laps of the pool. Taking a quick shower, she dried off, blew dry her hair into her usual bob and slipped on a turquoise green pair of silk pants with a loose white top.

She clutched the map of the resort that had been on the coffee table in the living room, and followed the directions to the day spa with the intention of making an appointment. As she made her way along outside corridors with marble flooring, she didn't pass one other person, and she couldn't help the comparison that sprang to mind.

While this might be a seven star resort, and the fittings and furnishing were of the highest quality, it seemed soulless, and didn't have the warm atmosphere that permeated Pentecost Island. Maybe it was simply because she felt at home there and had the support network of the girls who all looked out for each other.

'Boo!'

Sienna jumped and clutched her chest as Isla appeared from behind a marble column.

'I wondered where you'd got to. I was going to go and ask reception for your room number but they all seem so stuck up here, I didn't think they'd give it to me. I knew we'd run into each other somewhere. What have you been doing? Have you checked out the whole place? Isn't it amazing?' The Irish girl didn't draw breath as she continued to pepper Sienna with questions.

Finally Sienna put up her hand and grinned at her. 'How can I tell you what I've been doing if I can't get a word in?'

'I told you to tell me to button it if I got carried away, and I haven't spoken to a soul for two whole hours!' Isla chuckled. 'So I decided to go to the day spa and check it out. My God, did you see the prices in the compendium? I don't think I'll be having more than the basic treatment.'

'Okay to answer your question. I unpacked, and I had a swim. Then I decided to explore. It is very quiet here, I agree.' Sienna flicked a cheeky glance at Isla. 'I thought you might have still been with Mr Autopilot.'

'Nah, he was just a flirt. But you should have seen him checking you out when you walked away. You could have scored there if you'd wanted to. He wasn't interested in me.'

Sienna shook her head. 'No, thank you. I

don't want to score with anyone. I'm here to research, and have a rest, and then work at the course.'

'Just as well, because I checked out the talent around the bar at the far end of the pool on my first walk around. They're all over sixty, fat and hairy, and wearing gold chains.' Sienna grinned and Isla pulled a face. 'Unless you're looking for a sugar Daddy, the field is way too old, I suppose their wives are all shopping in the boutiques or having a beauty treatment.'

Sienna shook her head and put her arm though Isla's. 'Come on, let's go explore.'

It was impossible to be offended by Isla; she was full of fun and harmless, but her next words did put Sienna on edge.

'But never fear, if there is talent to be found, I will find it, and I did! Over the hill there is a construction site where they are building another accommodation wing near the rainforest, and oh, be still my beating heart, there were some buff builders there. I'd say we'll get to meet them when we're staying in the accommodation where the course is being held. That's the staff end of the island, so let's soak up this luxury while we're here!'

Sienna tensed. The last thing she wanted to look at was a buff builder and be reminded of Danny Riccardo. She stared over the balcony above the Bird of Paradise day spa and didn't speak.

'Look, I'm sorry, I do prattle on, but if you'd rather me leave you in peace, all you have to do is say the word, and I'll go.' Isla looked crestfallen and Sienna felt guilty for being aloof.

'No, of course not.' She let go of Isla's arm and smoothed her hands over her long pants. 'I'm just used to being quiet. I've always been that way.'

'Let me guess. Only child?'

'Yes.' Sienna swallowed and nodded. 'And boarding school.'

'Lucky you. I went to the village school in Dingle. That's where I learned to be loud. If you wanted to be heard so you could learn anything, you had to be.' Isla giggled. 'The poor teacher, can you imagine a class full of me? And then I went home to a little house filled with my five brothers, my parents and one set of grandparents. And the poor dears can't understand why I want to travel the world. "Why didn't you marry Tommy McEvoy when he asked you?" my mother said to me when they saw me off at the airport.'

'Your family sounds wonderful, 'Sienna said softly. 'And I'm so envious of your confidence.'

'They're not half bad. I miss them, you know. Paulie, Johnnie, Archie, Barrie and Frankie are all older than me, and only two of them are married. Me poor old Da was upset when Mum called me Isla. Broke the "ie" tradition. He wanted Mary!'

Sienna waited for her to draw breath, but it didn't happen.

'But hey, I'm envious of your elegance, and the way you look. I'd give anything to look like you do. You are so calm and serene. Maybe we can teach each other a few tricks.'

'Sounds like a plan. Now let's go and check

out this day spa.'

The three days spent as guests at the resort before their course began flew by. Sienna and Isla tried out a couple of the basic treatments in the day spa, and were both very impressed.

'Lots to learn, haven't we?' Isla said as they compared notes after the treatments.

They went shopping in the boutiques and Isla bought the basics of a new wardrobe with Sienna's help. But most of all they laughed as Isla taught Sienna the rudimentary facts about being self-confident.

On Saturday night, they chose the Italian restaurant for dinner. The tables were set with red checked tablecloths, and wine bottles with candles in the middle of the table. Dean Martin was crooning *It's Amore* as they were seated by a waiter with a fake Italian accent.

Isla rolled her eyes and grinned. 'I rest my case.'

'What?'

'It's all in the perception. The props.'

Sienna wasn't sure what her new friend meant, so Isla set an exercise for Sienna. As they sipped their wine Sienna's task was to look at each person in the restaurant, and tell Isla the background that she perceived they were from.

The more they drank, the sillier the conversation became, but Isla proved her point and Sienna took it on board.

'See, we each look at the people in here, and we both see something different, but none of it matters. What is important is what that person thinks of themself, and sweetie, that's what you have to work on.'

Sienna picked up the fine crystal glass and looked over her wine at Isla. 'So, tell me, how did you get your self-confidence? Was it something you had to work on?'

Isla shook her head. 'Lovey, the family I grew up in made me the way I am. There were ten of us in a tiny house, and we had to be loud and brash to be heard. Dinner around our table wasn't a posh affair.' Isla gestured with her fork at a couple on the other side of the restaurant. The woman was wearing a bronze silk dress, and the man a dinner suit. 'Now look at that pair. They're sitting there looking very confident and if I'm correct, they think they are better than many of the other guests in the restaurant. But'—she leaned forward and whispered—'why? What makes them better than everyone else? What makes them better than us?'

Sienna shook her head slowly. 'Nothing.'

'Exactly! Now what you have to do is tell yourself that that self-confidence that you give out in bucket loads is true, and not just a front you hide behind. You think you can do that, woman?'

Sienna sat straight in her chair. 'I'll give it my best shot.' As she said the words she knew she could do it, and she would do it.

'One more thing, you have to shed, before you pass the Isla O'Sullivan self-confidence course. And it's the hard one. You have to think deeply, and then you have to acknowledge who has done that damage to you. And then the fun begins when we deal with them.'

'But what if we're nowhere near them?' Sienna protested, thinking of her father in that huge draughty house on the lake in Switzerland.

Isla leaned forward and tapped her nose. 'But lovey, I'm Irish and I can show you the magic, and we can do it from here.'

Sienna burst out laughing and Isla put one hand on her chest. 'Now, it's hurting me you are. How can a girl help her friend if she laughs at her?' Isla leaned forward and lowered her voice. 'You have to tell me who did this number on you, and then we deal with it. A couple of candles, a lock of hair, and we burn some notes and you'll be as right as rain, Sienna Marino!'

Sienna leaned back. One thing Isla had taught her was to take herself less seriously. They were quiet as the fake Italian waiter placed two steaming bowls of spaghetti marinara in front of them.

Isla ploughed straight in as Sienna unfolded her napkin and laid it on her lap. She picked up the silver fork, as Isla sucked a piece of spaghetti in.

Finally Sienna shook her head. 'It's no use. No matter. It's no use, I can't do it.'

'Okay, I'll lance the wound for you myself. Figuratively speaking, that is. Who was the person who did this to you? The person who made you believe that you're not good enough?'

'It was my father,' Sienna mumbled. 'But I can't blame him. It was as much my fault as his.'

'Ah, that's a bit harder than a past love who broke your heart.'

Sienna looked down. 'There was one of them too. Not long ago.'

'We've got our work cut out, girlfriend, but we've got ten days to work on you.' Isla leaned forward and her gaze was intense. 'If you put your trust in me, I guarantee you that the Sienna who leaves this island will be a different—and stronger—person than the one she is now. So, do you trust me?'

Sienna nodded slowly. 'Strangely, Isla O' Sullivan, I do.'

Chapter 19

Danny

Danny was up bright and early on Sunday morning to travel to Esculanta Island. The Air BnB was in walking distance of the marina, and he'd already checked out the launch that would take him out to the island. Surprisingly, his mood was upbeat—he'd had a good break at Port Douglas and had got his head in order and he was looking forward to starting afresh. It was time to put the past behind him, and move on. There was one thing he'd like to do, but knew it was impossible.

He would have liked to have known that Sienna was all right. He would never forget the shock on her face when he'd climbed back into the boat, his nose dripping with blood.

It hadn't been the injury that had shocked her; he knew it had been Renzo's loud comment about him having a wife. All he could hope for was that Sienna's friends on the island would rally around her; he'd seen them in action, and they were a tight support group. He was going to have to try hard to get over his feelings for her. He was going to steer clear of women for a long time. But he would have liked to have spoken to her one more time and told her his story.

It was time to focus on his new job; Danny had no doubt he had the skills listed by the recruitment service when he had applied, and once he had provided evidence of his trade qualification to the project manager on the island, he should be clear to start work tomorrow.

Locking the door behind him and dropping the key into the return box, he headed for the marina to catch the launch to the island.

##

To save time on arrival at the worksite, the construction company had a temporary counter on the wharf on the mainland. Danny was early and was first at the desk.

'Daniel Riccardo, carpenter,' he answered when asked for his name and the position he was filling.

The man at the desk ran his finger down a list and checked Danny's name off. 'You have a copy of your tickets with you?'

Danny nodded and slipped them from his wallet.

Another four ticks on the list.

'Excellent, thank you.' His name was crossed off and the guy handed him a name tag, and an envelope. 'You're in the staff accommodation on the eastern side of the island. Please read this and sign your agreement.' He slid a single page across the desk.

Danny widened his eyes as he read the conditions of employment. No visiting the resort, no drinking at the bar or eating at the restaurant, and no fraternising with the guests. He had no problem with it, but it was not what he'd expected. He signed the paper. 'I was expecting a construction site. I didn't know the resort was already open,' he commented as he passed the form back over.

'Does that create a problem for you?' the guy asked. Danny looked at his name tag. 'No, Jim.

No problem. I wasn't aware there would be guests there, that's all. I didn't know it was already open.'

'It's totally separate,' Jim replied. 'You'll be working on the new hotel wing in the centre of the island. The existing resort is on the western side, and the staff and builders' accommodation, and the training centre is on the east. It's quite a large island, and the guests are discouraged from going beyond the resort fence.'

'Fair enough.'

'In your envelope, you'll find the details of your accommodation and the arrangements for meals and leisure activities on the island. He nodded to Danny. 'You can board the launch now. I think you'll be pleasantly surprised.'

As Danny move away towards the boat, he noticed a queue had formed behind him. To his dismay, there was a large group of women standing at the back and they were looking his way and obviously talking about him. He put his head down and headed onboard, choosing a corner seat at the back. He rolled his jacket up and put it between his head and the window. It was almost a three hour trip out to the island; he'd sleep rather than get caught up in conversations.

He was pleased when a guy took the seat beside him, gave him a brief nod and immediately opened his laptop. The group of women went upstairs to the open deck, chattering and giggling as they went.

God, he was getting cynical for a bloke his age.

***

Sienna had been woken at seven-thirty by the phone beside her bed. She and Isla had had a late night last night—after dinner, they had watched a show and then gone to the small cinema behind the restaurant to watch the latest Liam Hemsworth movie.

Isla had chuckled. 'One of my reasons for coming to Australia. How about you?'

Sienna had shaken her head. 'No. I'm here to work. No time for that sort of thing.'

'Well, you won't have been disappointed

because there's not been one decent man to look at over the weekend.'

'I haven't been looking.

'I noticed,' Isla had said drily. 'We're going to work on that too.'

Now Sienna rolled over and reached for the phone. 'Hello?'

'Ms Marino? It's Andie from reception here. You are checking out this morning and we have no travel arrangements in the system for you. Were you taking the sea plane back to the mainland, or the launch? I need to generate a ticket for you.'

'Ah.' Sienna hesitated as she tried to wake up and gather her thoughts. 'I'm not going back today. I'm moving across to the training centre for a course.'

'I wasn't aware of that. Just one moment.' Silence and then the clicking of a keyboard. 'My apologies, Ms Marino. I see that you and Ms O'Sullivan are both moving over to the training centre.' There was a crisp tone in the voice now, almost as though they were in trouble.

Sienna sat up and pushed her hair back with one hand as she leaned on the silk pillowcase. 'There are regulations about moving between sites.' Definitely a frosty tone now. 'You can both have a late check out, and then if you come down to reception at eleven a.m. we will transport you over so that you arrive at the same time as the launch with the other course attendees.'

Sienna went to speak but the call disconnected; she pulled a face, reception wouldn't be getting a good score on the evaluation form. Course attendees were obviously second class citizens from the resort staff point of view. She snuggled back down in the bed. If she had a late checkout, she would make the most of it with a lie in. She had a feeling the next ten days would be very busy.

Busy was good. Busy would help her get into the right headspace before she went back to Pentecost Island.

A head space and a location where Danny wouldn't be anymore.

Sienna turned her head into the pillow and for the first time in two days gave in to tears.

Chapter 20

Sienna

Isla was waiting at reception when Sienna stepped out of the lift. Her new friend was wearing one of the new outfits she'd bought with Sienna's help.

'Morning, lovey.' Her shrill voice filled the foyer and heads turned as Sienna crossed the marble floor.

'You look lovely, Isla,' she said, and meant it. Isla had pulled her loose curls back and subdued them in a French roll.

'I did until you walked across.' Her grin was cheeky. 'My elegance fades in your shadow.'

'As my self-confidence does in yours.' Sienna nudged her. 'Did you get the frosty call from Andie?'

'I did,' Isla said mournfully, but loudly. 'No longer are we guests to be pampered.'

The receptionist looked over at them and raised her eyebrows. 'Your luggage has been taken out, and your transport will be here shortly, if you would like to wait on the seat outside.'

Sienna glanced back at the rude woman as they headed to the doors. 'She wouldn't last five minutes on Pentecost Island. One of Pippa's rules is perfect and appropriate behaviour with the guests at all times.'

'We are no longer guests. But I do like the sound of your island, and your Pippa.'

'We were tested a couple of months back with a new arrival who rubbed everyone up the wrong way, but Odessa turned out to be a good person. We never know what baggage people carry, do we?'

'No, we don't.'

Sienna glanced at Isla. Her tone had held a rare note of bitterness.

'Any jobs coming up on your island?'

Sienna looked at her as she wondered, *No, it wasn't the right time to say anything.* She'd only known Isla for three days and as much as she enjoyed her company, she'd have to see what sort of therapist she was before she mentioned any jobs that might be coming up.

'You'll be the first to know,' she replied. 'You'd love the island and the girls. It's a pretty special place.'

'You never know, I might come for a holiday. Depends if I get a job out of this course. I have heard that therapists who have completed Madame Eleve's course are in high demand.'

'Fingers crossed,' Sienna said. 'Look, here comes our chariot. She stifled a giggle as a buggy the same as those on Hamo came around the corner.

'And here was I thinking we'd have a limousine,' Isla said with a chuckle.

##

The ride across to the other side of the island took them along a winding road with an overhanging canopy of rainforest trees. Brightly coloured birds jumped from branch to branch above them, squawking as the buggy disturbed them. Like the rest of the island, the road was clear of leaves and bird droppings and Sienna smothered a smile, remembering Eliza's pooper scooper story.

It had been true; she and Isla had checked it out. They'd also checked out the bare-chested waiters around the pool and the hot towels that were hand delivered for their comfort.

'We had a good holiday, didn't we?' she said with a smile as they approached the end of the road.

'I did, and by the look of you, you did too. You look much more relaxed than you did when you got on the plane.'

The buggy driver turned around to speak to them. 'I'll drop you off where you register your arrival, but I'll take your bags to your rooms. Might be a bit of a wait, girls, it's a large group, plus there's new workmen coming over for the week on this morning's launch. There's a coffee shop there, so I'd suggest making that your first stop.'

'Thank you.' Isla patted his shoulder as they left the buggy. 'I'll be recommending you for a staff recognition award. It's a pleasure to have someone friendly.'

With a smile and a wave, he headed off to a building at the end of a circular drive.

'That must be our accommodation. It doesn't look too bad.' Sienna stared at the four-storey building ahead. Each room appeared to have a balcony that overlooked the sea, and the gardens were colourful and well looked after.

'I guess they have to keep it looking on a par with the rest of the place in case any guests wander over here. There's the coffee shop. Looks like we're first to arrive.'

As they crossed the paved area to the small coffee shop, Sienna spotted a large boat coming across the small bay. 'Look, there's the launch now. Let's get a coffee and see where we have to register.'

'Over there, Sienna.' Isla pointed to a separate building next to the coffee shop. 'It says. Madame Eleve course attendees register here. And there's a spare table right near it. You grab the table, I'll get our coffees.'

'Espresso, double shot, please,' Sienna said

as she moved across to the table. She sat down and watched the launch as it headed for the wharf.

Very different to Jiminy's boat that did the run to Pentecost Island. This was a two deck boat with an open seating area on the upper deck as well as a cabin.

Sienna was surprised to see how many passengers were on the launch. There was a large group of women sitting in the open air on the top deck. As she watched the boat manoeuvre in, it was obvious that the bottom deck was full too. There were faces at each window. As the boat got closer her breath caught and she put her hand to her mouth.

'I got us a piece of carrot cake to share too,' Isla said as she sat down. The girl in there's a sweetie. She's bringing it out. Real cups too.' Her eyes narrowed as she looked at Sienna. 'You okay? You're a bit pale.'

Sienna looked back at the launch, but there was no one at the window where she could have sworn she'd seen Danny.

She nodded. 'I'm okay. Just losing the plot.'

'Join me, girlfriend, I lost it years ago.'

Sienna kept her attention on the boat as the coffee and cake was brought out to them.

'This is Sienna,' Isla said.

'Hi, welcome to the best side of the island. I'm Frannie.'

'Hi, Frannie.' Sienna glanced at her briefly with a quick smile, keeping her attention on the passengers as they disembarked. Isla chattered away and as the last group came off the boat, Sienna let out the breath she'd been holding. It had been her imagination.

Frannie went back inside and Sienna pulled her coffee over to her.

'Go you halvies in the cake?' Isla asked, spoon poised.

'No, thanks, I'm not hungry.'

'You okay, lovey? You looked like you'd seen a ghost before.'

Sienna flopped back into the chair. 'I thought I almost had for a moment. I mean, not a ghost, just someone I don't want to see.'

'That wouldn't be the cause of the broken heart you mentioned the other night?'

She nodded. 'Yes, it's still pretty raw. Only happened a few days before I came up here. I'm still a bit fragile.'

'Tell Aunty Isla all about it. I always wanted to be one of those agony aunts that people wrote to in the women's mags.'

'No, there's no need. It's all over and it was my imagination. I was seeing things.'

Isla picked up her coffee and looked over Sienna's shoulder. 'Seeing things or not, there's some definite talent heading this way. Check them out. I think they're coming into the coffee shop.'

Sienna pulled a face. 'I'll drink my coffee while you check them out.'

'I've always been a sucker for a man in a suit. Always looks like he has a bit of class, but then you shouldn't stereotype and make assumptions, should you?'

Sienna half switched off, as Isla continued

her constant talking. She didn't often seem to expect an answer. She looked down at her coffee, and then picked up her spoon to stir the chocolate in.

'Now the one with the curly black hair with him looks like that pretend Italian waiter we had the other night. They're coming this way.'

Sienna's neck prickled and she sat still, staring into her cup as a shadow passed the table. Finally looking up, she saw the back of a man in a suit as he went into the coffee shop. She looked back at Isla who was staring past her shoulder.

Sienna held her breath as a shadow crossed the table and then stopped. She looked down at a pair of work boots. Work boots she had seen before.

Her eyes travelled slowly up a fine set of tanned muscular legs.

Legs that she recognised.

She held her breath as she lifted her gaze and her vision blurred as her heart began to thump erratically. She stared into a beautiful face.

A face that was imprinted on her heart.

'Sienna?' Danny was staring at her with his mouth open.

Isla stood, and came around to Sienna's side of the table. Her eyes held concern. 'Time we were heading, lovey. There's quite a queue over at the registration office now.'

Sienna moved her eyes from Danny's face and looked down at the table.

'Isla, you finish your cake and coffee. I'm sure they'll wait for us to register. I have a conversation to have.' She was very proud of her firm voice. 'It'll only take a few minutes.'

Sienna glanced over at the launch wondering how long it was before it left. With Danny Riccardo on it.

The look of hopeful expectation on his face fuelled her growing anger even more.

'Danny, walk with me please. We need to talk.'

Chapter 21

Danny

When Danny had seen the woman with the auburn hair sitting at the coffee table, his heart had kicked, and then he'd chastised himself for seeing Sienna everywhere he went.

How long was this going to last?

She was sitting beside a slim girl with dark hair who was staring at him.

'A word of warning, Dan.' Eric, the guy he'd sat next to on the trip over—the architect who designed the new wing—leaned over and dropped his voice. 'Don't get involved with any of the course participants while they're on the island. There's been a few guys lose their jobs over it. The construction firm are pretty hard taskmasters and expectations are a bit over the top.

'No fear of that from me,' he said.

'Good to meet you. I hope it works out for you.' Eric nodded and hurried across to the coffee shop and disappeared inside.

As Danny got closer to the table, his heart

kicked up even more when he saw the graceful neck above the white silk shirt. He knew that skin and that neck and that hair.

It was Sienna.

His first thought was that she'd found out he was coming to the island and had organised to meet him.

Hope surged through him, until she lifted her eyes and her icy glare raked him. Twin spots of red coloured her usually fair cheeks, and her eyes glittered.

Then he remembered that no one knew he was coming here, so there was no way she could have known.

'Danny, walk with me please. We need to talk.'

She stood and her chair scraped on the pavers. 'Now.'

The girl standing beside her looked worried. 'I'll wait for you here, Sienna.'

'No, you go and join the queue, Isla. I won't be long.'

The course.

The penny dropped. This was the course Sienna had found out about last Sunday when they were on Hamo. The course with the tropical resort on the front of the brochure. Danny bit back the groan that threatened to spill out.

What were the chances of that? Out of all of the jobs he'd considered, how the hell did he end up applying for and getting one on the very island where her course was being held? And what were the chances of her being here the same day he arrived?

Sienna's low heels clicked on the road beneath their feet as she led him towards a road that seem to lead to a rainforest. As they reached the corner, he could see it was a wide paved road, overhung with a canopy of trees.

'This is far enough,' she said. 'No one can hear us here.'

'So?' He put his hands on his hip and his laptop case swung around.

'So?' Her voice was vicious. 'Is that all you

have to say?'

'At this stage, yes, until I hear what you want to talk to me about.'

'What I want to talk to you about?' Her chest was heaving as her voice got louder. 'I'll tell you what I want to talk to you about! What sort of an ego do you have to follow me here? Who told you? Did Pippa tell your sleazeball brother I was on Esculanta Island?'

'I—'

'How dare you, Danny? Isn't it enough that you're married? What does your poor wife have to say about you chasing after me? I cannot believe you are here. I want you to get on that launch and go away and leave me in peace. I never want to see you again.'

As she spoke the hooter of the launch boomed, and the roar of engines reached them as it pulled away from the wharf.

'Looks like it's too late.' He couldn't help himself, but Danny was starting to get angry.

'You planned all this, didn't you?'

'Yeah, sure I did. I made sure that you were sitting in that seat so you could see me as soon as I got off the boat. Wake up to yourself, Sienna, and stop being so selfish and one-eyed. You wouldn't let me explain myself to you the other night. It's about time you got out of your fantasy world and listened.'

'Fantasy world? How dare you!'

Before he saw it coming, Sienna had lifted her hand and slapped his face. But his reflexes were fast, and he caught her hand in his on the way down. His cheek was stinging where her hand had landed but he ignored it.

'I'll tell you how I dare to. I left my job on Pentecost Island so you didn't have to see me. I told my brother to shove his job, and I left my home. I was overjoyed when the woman my family arranged for me to marry went back to Italy. I was ecstatic when I filed for divorce. But you didn't care enough to wait and listen and hear any of that, did you? You thought the worst of me and gave me no chance. So, you know what? I don't care what you think of me now. I don't want to have anything to do with you. I've started a new life and you have no place in it. I have a four week contract here and I'm going to give it a go. I had no idea that you were here. If I had I would have gone in the other direction, as far as I could, and very fast. You showed me no respect, and you gave me no trust, so you can now do whatever it is you're here to do, but don't you come near me. Is that clear?'

'Very. Now let go of me.'

He dropped her hand.

She turned on her heel and walked away, leaving him standing in the shadow of a huge mango tree. His heart was thumping and his head was pounding.

And God help him, he couldn't help watching her as she strode away.

She even did that bloody elegantly.

But it was the yearning that filled him that pissed Danny off more than anything.

Chapter 22
Sienna

By the time she had settled into the shared room with Isla, Sienna had achieved a measure of calm. She couldn't believe she'd slapped Danny's face; she had no idea where that had come from. Her temperament had always been calm, no matter how much her father had goaded her. The incident today had been the culmination of her rage; she'd become so angry she hadn't even realised she'd slapped him until he'd grabbed her hand.

Embarrassment sat uncomfortably in her stomach the whole time they'd registered for the course and then sat through an introductory talk before she and Isla had been given their room keys. The rest of the day was theirs to read some course materials and explore their side of the island. They had access to small catamarans and kayaks, and a long stretch of beach that was for staff only.

Sienna was conscious of Danny being close by; she'd seen the workers go into a room in the same building for what she assumed was their orientation. All she wanted was to be somewhere else. Somewhere she could climb into bed and pull the sheets over her head, and forget what Danny had said.

She'd made assumptions about him, and she'd judged him without knowing the facts. Worse than that, he'd listened to her secrets, he had been kind and he hadn't judged her. She had not given him the same courtesy, without knowing the facts.

Tears pricked at her eyes as Sienna listened to a boring woman drone on about what the course would cover for the next ten days. Her interest level was zero. She was beginning to doubt that she had the staying power to be here and do the course, and then she remembered the huge amount that Eliza had paid so she could, and she knew she had to do it. Isla must have sensed her turmoil because she was unusually quiet and at one stage when Sienna teared up, she reached over and squeezed her hand.

When the woman—Madame Eleve by all accounts—finally stopped talking about herself and how wonderful this course was because she'd created it, Sienna was ready to go to her room and crash.

She must have looked wrecked, because when they stood, Isla took her elbow and guided her outside.

'It's very regimented, isn't it,' she whispered. 'Nothing like I was expecting. In fact the whole island is a bit—I don't know, almost like something out of a horror movie.'

Sienna managed to pull herself out of her funk. 'It's going to be okay. It's had all those excellent reviews.'

'Hmm. We'll see. Now did you hear what she said? We're to go to our rooms and rest and read, and then come back in two hours for dinner. Are you okay with that? You have to eat, you know, lovey.'

Sienna smiled as Isla looked at her with concern. 'You're a good friend, Isla. And yes, I know. I won't be a coward. I'll come to dinner. Even though I know Danny will be there. It's the dining area for everyone on this side of the island.'

'Well, chin up, lovey. Come and make yourself even more beautiful, and we'll go slay them!'

Sienna almost managed a laugh, but she couldn't hold back her smile.

***

Danny

Danny had thought it was impossible to feel any worse than he had when he had taken Sienna back to the island after Renzo had spilled the beans on him being married, but after the tirade he'd unleashed on Sienna in the forest this afternoon, he felt dreadful. Guilt and regret vied for top spot, and he sat in the orientation session, completely unaware of what was going on around him.

Luckily the guy beside him nodded to him as the speaker turned the microphone off. 'Coming for a beer, mate? I think we need one after that.'

'Sounds good. I switched off. What did I miss?'

The guy laughed and held out his hand. 'I'm

Brad. Don't worry. I picked up the good stuff. Where the bar and the restaurant are. The staff ones, that is. Stick with me, and I'll show you the way.'

The bar beside the open dining area was large and already half filled with men and women. Danny had a furtive look around, and once he was sure that a certain redhead wasn't in the room, he let himself relax. He and Brad sat at a large table by themselves and chatted about their first impressions of the island.

'I'm a bit disappointed to be honest,' Danny said.

Maybe it was because he was used to Pentecost and the vibe there, but so far, he wasn't impressed. He'd had it good on Pentecost Island. Not just because Sienna was there to talk to, but he'd also enjoyed working with the rest of the staff; the atmosphere was always happy.

If he was honest, even he and Renzo worked well together.

With a sigh he looked up as he caught the flash of red he'd been waiting for. No, it wasn't fair to call the gorgeous colour red.

Sienna and her friend were standing in the doorway. He felt the instant her eyes settled on him, and looked down at his beer. She could decide whether to go or stay. It didn't matter to him.

Oh yes, it does, a little voice pounded at him.

Okay, so it did. He'd like to sit and talk to her, and ignore the past week.

Danny didn't resent the way Sienna had spoken to him. Hell, he could understand exactly where she was coming from. He could even forgive her for slapping him. Finding out he was married after he had kissed her like he had last Sunday must have been a shock to her.

There had been times over the past three years when he'd woken up in a cold sweat—Lucia in the next room she had never ventured from—when he'd not been able to believe he was married. It remained a shock to him almost three years later.

So he couldn't blame Sienna for her reaction. The sad part of it was, he really liked her and that day together on Hamo had shown him it could be much more.

So much more. He really cared for her. He'd loved talking to her, and spending time with her. Even watching her potter around her day spa had given him pleasure. Folding towels and arranging the flowers; he had been a sucker for anything she did.

He refused to let himself think of that afternoon on Hamo, when they could have very easily become a lot more than friends.

He'd blown it now, and he just had to get on with the four weeks on the island, and let her get on with her life.

It was too late.

'Another beer, mate?' he asked Brad.

Chapter 23
Pippa

Sienna had only been gone for four days when it became very obvious to me that her replacement was not going to make it. Jen had whined almost nonstop since she'd come to the island, and I was over it.

The hut was too far from everyone else.

There were too many bookings in the day.

The old house was not suitable accommodation. Her list of complaints was never ending.

On the fifth morning she was on the island, and my phone rang for the third time, Rafe looked at me, with sympathy in his eyes.

'You're going to send her back to Hamo, aren't you, sweetheart?'

'Am I that obvious?' I let out a satisfied sigh as my husband put his arms around me.

'Only to someone who loves you,' he said.

'Sure makes me appreciate the excellent

staff we have here.'

The sky was dark with grey clouds and a brisk wind was blowing from the north. It had rained on and off for the past few days, and I was frustrated that it was holding up the work on our new pool. Renzo had talked to the designer, the plans had gone to council and we'd manged to get them fast tracked, but I had no control over the weather.

It hadn't been a good week. Nat and Nate had gone down to Brisbane to look at a new reservation system we were thinking of installing. Yesterday's meat delivery for the restaurant had gone astray and Angus had to change the menu at short notice. The whining beautician had been the last straw.

Half an hour later, I walked back up the hill and a tiny spurt of jealousy went through me as I spotted Odessa sitting outside with Rafe. I knew I had nothing to worry about, but she still held a place in his heart from before I had known him.

I pushed it away.

'Hey, Odessa. I haven't seen you for a few days.'

Her smile was natural and warm, and I realised how unfair I was being. I'd had my friends from before Rafe, and I shouldn't worry about his. I should know to be secure in his love, but sometimes my past baggage made itself known.

My husband reached up and took my hand as I stopped behind his chair.

'Ready for a coffee, love?' he asked.

'I am.'

'I'll get you one. And Odessa bought cake from Cherry.'

'Hummingbird cake,' Odessa said.

'Oh, yum, that has just improved my day,' I said.

'That's good,' Odessa said with a nervous smile. I was surprised; I hadn't seen her less than composed before.

'Why good?' I asked.

She swallowed and moistened her lips with the tip of her tongue. 'I wanted to ask your opinion on something.'

I tipped my head to the side. Even after almost two years I still didn't have a complete handle on being the boss. It didn't come naturally, and this week had made me wonder if I really wanted to be in charge of a resort that was growing faster than we'd ever imagined.

'Fire away.'

'Well'—she toyed with the fringe on the edge of her skirt—'when I went over to Hamo the other day, I got talking to a couple of the designers in the jewellery outlets. I just happened to have a few of my pieces with me, and I was surprised that they thought they were good.'

I smiled. 'I'm not surprised at all. You're very talented.'

'You really think so, you're not just saying that?'

'I do.'

'Okay.' She took a deep breath. 'How would you feel about me having an exhibition here? Just a small function in the restaurant, and then I'd leave some of my work on display there. Of course, I'd pay for the catering and any costs that came from it, and I'd give you a percentage of any sales I made. I'd much rather have it here where it's familiar than over on Hamo.' She put her hands on the table and stopped fidgeting. 'Take a while to think about it, talk it over with Rafe. There's no rush.'

As I looked at her, Rafe came out with the coffee and three slices of cake on a plate.

'I don't have to think.'

Odessa's face fell. 'Oh, it doesn't matter. Don't worry, it was just an idea.'

I leaned forward and put my hand on hers. 'Odessa, I think it's a great idea. Just the sort of thing we need here to put us on the map.' My advertising brain kicked in. 'We could advertise in the national papers, and social media. When do you want to have it?'

I was surprised when Odessa jumped up and did a happy dance. 'Oh my God, you want to do it!'

Rafe trailed his fingers along my shoulder as he walked past, and I took that as approval.

'Let's talk dates,' I said. 'And then I can draft some ads.'

##

A couple of hours later, Odessa had gone back down to the house, and Rafe and I were sitting together in the swing chair watching the water. I leaned back against him and closed my eyes.

'You've finally accepted Odessa,' he said softly brushing his lips over my forehead.

'She's lovely. And she's really settled in on the island.'

'I'm pleased,' was all he said.

'It's been a tough week. I'll be pleased when Sienna comes back. I really hope she does.'

'You think she mightn't?'

I finally gave voice to what had been bugging me all day. 'I was talking to Renzo at the pool site this morning, and he told me where Danny's gone. He's not supposed to know, but the foreman of the company knew Renzo and rang him when he saw Danny's surname.'

'And?'

'He's working on Esculanta Island.'

'Oh dear. That could be interesting,' Rafe said. 'Do you think you should call her?'

'Probably too late. They'll be there by now.'

Rafe settled me comfortably against him. 'You know what? It might not be a bad thing, throwing them together like that away from everything they know. They obviously had a spark going.'

'So you think I should just let it run its natural course?' I asked.

Rafe's arms went around me. 'I do, sweetheart. You have to learn you can't fix everything yourself.'

Chapter 24
Sienna

It hadn't taken long for Sienna's anger to morph into guilt, and then the resultant plummet of her new self-confidence followed soon after.

Isla sat next to her at the long dining table. They had come in late and the only seats left had been at a table for two right next to where Danny was sitting at a large table with five other men.

Sienna had taken a bowl of salad from the buffet and was twirling her fork in it. She'd sat at the side of the table so her back was to Danny, and then worried that he would be looking at her.

Isla leaned forward over the bowl of pasta and whispered. 'Relax, sweetie. He's not even looking this way. He's talking to the others at the table.'

'Thank you, you're a mind reader.'

'I am, and I'm going to play agony aunt here. You, my dear have ten huge days of work ahead of you, and I want to see you eat properly and sleep well. Or you are going to fall in a heap. You told me your boss paid for this. Do you want to let her down?'

Sienna shook her head. 'No, I don't want to. I won't let Pippa and Eliza down.'

'So what do you have to do?'

'I'm going to eat my dinner.' She looked across at Isla and put on as much of a smile as she could muster. 'Even if it chokes me.'

'And then we will have pudding,' Isla said.

'Pudding? What's that?' Sienna frowned. 'What are you going to make me do?'

Isla burst out laughing and heads turned. 'I guess you call it *torte* or something. A sweet after our dinner. And I saw a big pot of rice pudding over there. Not the sort of thing we were offered in the seven star resort, was it?'

'I'll look forward to trying it,' Sienna said softly. 'I've never had rice pudding, and, yes, the food was awful at the resort. I can't wait to tell Pippa. If that was seven star our island is ten!'

Isla laughed again. 'That's a girl. Good to see some life coming back into you.' I was worried you were going to bail on me.'

'No. I'm staying. Even if Danny is staying too.'

'What did you say to him this afternoon. He looked shattered when he came back.'

Sienna shook her head and lowered her voice even more. 'I said some pretty horrible things. I think I'm going to have to apologise. I was out of line, but the shock of seeing him here made me see red. I thought he'd followed me here, but he didn't know I was here.'

'Are you sure? Is he being honest?'

She nodded. 'I believe him. He was as shocked to see me as I was to see him.'

'This might sound silly, but what are the chances of you both turning up here, unknown to each other, at the same time.'

'I'd say about one in a million.' It was all Sienna could do, not to turn around and look at the man they were talking about.

'I'm a great believer in fate, lovey. Do you think fate has stepped in here?'

'What do you mean?' Sienna sighed as there was movement beside their table and Danny walked past with three other men, but he didn't even look her way. 'He's still angry with me.'

'And that's part of it. I have some very strong ideas about how we end up with our soulmates,' Isla said, her expression more serious than Sienna had seen up until now. 'I know I'm looking too hard, because I want to be part of a couple, and I always make the wrong choices. But never have I met the person who I knew I was destined to be with. So, when we've moved on, I've never cared very much. And I've gone looking again.'

'You're saying Danny is my soul mate?' Sienna propped her chin in her hand on the table.

'Has there been really strong emotion between you? I don't want to get too personal, but even the anger between you today is a sign of a connection. It wouldn't have been there without there being a connection.' Isla jumped to her feet. 'Stay there while I get our pudding, and when I come back I want you to tell me every emotion you've shared with that man.' She turned as she went to walk to the *bain maries*. 'And to make it even stranger, if you're not a believer, we were destined to meet so I could help you on your path.'

Sienna sat there with her mouth open as Isla walked away. She looked down at her salad bowl, surprised to see it empty.

Closing her eyes, she thought back over the past few months that she'd been on the island.

***

Danny was restless. The guys he'd sat with at dinner had invited him back to the bar, but he'd excused himself saying he was going to have an early night. He couldn't bear the thought that Sienna might be there, and he couldn't go near her, couldn't talk to her, couldn't touch her.

Not because she was angry at him, but because it wasn't the right thing to do. He went back to his room—pleased that they all had single rooms—and changed out of his work clothes and boots. Putting on a pair of boardshorts and a T-shirt, he decided to walk along the beach. The weather had turned, but despite the wind and the scudding grey clouds, it was still warm. There was a compendium in his room, and according to the rules, swimming was not permitted at the beach. There was a small staff pool behind the bar for exercise, and a gym adjacent to the conference room where they'd met this afternoon.

He pulled the door shut behind him and turned his face to the sky, letting the first few drops of rain hit his face. It was cool and refreshing, and made him feel slightly better. When Sienna had calmed down, he intended to seek her out and apologise. As he stepped onto the narrow sandy beach, he could see a light a few hundred metres away. According to the rule book—and there seemed to be a lot of rules on the island, that was as far as staff could go.

The rain was light as he walked and by the time he reached the end of the beach and turned around the sky had cleared. As he got closer to the accommodation buildings, he could see a lone figure sitting on the seat where the path went down to the beach. His heart kicked as hope took hold of him, but he told himself it wouldn't be Sienna. There were thirty other women on this island, and she wouldn't be sitting out here alone.

Or would she?

No, she would be in the bar talking to her new friend.

Danny put his head down and stepped from the beach onto the path and kept walking. The bar was lit up, and he could hear music coming from the building.

'Danny.'

The soft voice stopped him in his tracks.

'Can we talk, please?'

He put his hands in his pockets and walked over to the bench seat where Sienna was sitting. She sat up straight as he approached and the wind caught her hair. She reached up and pushed it back and a whiff of her fragrance reached him.

Danny took a deep breath and fought to think of the right words to say. He wanted to talk to her too, but he didn't want to frighten her, or hurt her any more than he already had.

Without saying a word, he sat at the other end of the seat, taking his hands from his pockets. He leaned back taking another deep breath.

They sat there quietly as the wind gusted in from the sea.

Finally Danny found the courage to speak. 'We can. I just want to say how sorry I am for what I said this afternoon. I was cruel, and I didn't mean one word of it.'

Sienna moved along the seat so she was closer to him, and Danny almost groaned.

'I am sorry too. What I said was unforgiveable, and I hope you can forget everything I said. And I hope you can forgive me for not trusting you. I knew you were a good person, and I should have let you tell me your story. Especially after I dumped all my baggage on you.'

Danny looked down, unable to believe what

he was hearing and unable to believe that Sienna had moved closer and had reached for his hand. She laced her fingers through his.

'Why?' he said. 'What changed your mind?'

'Advice from a very wise woman. Advice that I should have known instinctively. Even though we began as friends, Danny, I think it became very clear to both of us that there was something there. You held back because of your situation, and I held back because I don't know—or I didn't know—how to trust. Can we start again?'

'As friends?' he asked carefully.

'I believe the right people come into our lives when they're meant to. Up until you, it was a friendship level, the girls who've helped me. Eliza and Pippa, and now my new and very wise friend Isla has made me see the truth.'

'Up until me?' he said carefully reaching for her other hand.

'I care about you, Danny, and if all you want is friendship, I can accept that. I know you're not in a position for more than that.'

Danny couldn't put into words the joy that was coursing through him. Finally he stood and pulled Sienna to her feet. 'I am now, and I'm finding it very hard to speak. Can I show you what I need to say?'

Sienna stepped into his arms.

***

The words that she had ready for Isla when she had come back with their rice pudding ran through Sienna's mind as Danny held her close. She whispered the words as he held her. 'Friendship, caring, laughter, hope, inspiration, joy, amusement, serenity, and maybe even love.'

Danny put his cheek against hers as she whispered. She could feel his smile against her skin. His fingers smoothed her hair as he held her close. For the first time in her life, she knew she was safe and happy. Reaching up with one hand, she brushed his face with trembling fingers. 'You're a good man, Danny.'

'What were those words about?' he asked.

'All of the emotions we've shared so far.'

226

'You are a beautiful woman,' he said. 'How could I not feel those emotions when I'm with you.?'

Sienna looked up and saw her own need mirrored in those dark brown eyes. She lifted her face and touched her lips to his. Danny's hold tightened, but he lifted his head away from her kiss.

'Wait. I haven't told you the best news yet. In about a week, I will no longer be married, and the record will say I have never been married.'

She widened her eyes and his smile grew. 'Thanks to a kind old lawyer, and a declaration of nullity, the record will show I've never been married. It's a long story but not one I want to tell you tonight. Tonight is for kissing you, my Sienna.'

Chapter 25
Pippa - Ten days later

Sienna had stayed away for an extra week after her course finished but she promised that she was coming back. None of us knew what had happened, but Rafe looked smug when I told him how happy she'd sounded when she'd called.

'Told you they would work it out,' he said.

'You're jumping to conclusions,' I said as I rolled over and put my head on his chest. We had slept in, and it was time we were up. I had a big day ahead, but I always found it hard to leave Rafe in bed.

'I'll make a bet with you that she and Danny have sorted it out.' Rafe ran his fingers down my spine and I decided I definitely was getting out of bed.

'What makes you so sure?'

'Because I write stories and I like a happy ending,' he said, making me smile.

'How about a happy ending now?' I said cheekily as my fingers started a journey down his chest.

##

An hour later, I was running around trying to get ready for an interview I'd forgotten I had at the house at a quarter past ten. Eliza had insisted that I interview this guy for the lifeguard position at the pool. Apparently she and Phillipe had met him, and decided he would be perfect for the position. Renzo's guys had already done the excavation for the pool, and the logistics of getting an excavator over, and then to the location on the point where the pool was to be located had been a stressful exercise.

The guy, Zachary Johnson, was coming over with Jiminy on the ten o'clock launch.

Tonight was the staff Christmas party, and we'd closed the restaurant. Angus had called a couple of casual chefs in to cater as well as doing a buffet dinner at the old house for the guests.

'I'm going now, Rafe.' I called, grabbing a piece of toast, and my coffee. 'I'll be back for lunch.'

Rafe came out of the study. 'I'll walk down with you. I want to talk to Tess about a reservation for a couple of friends who emailed me overnight.'

I laughed as we headed to the gate. 'More Odessas?'

He bumped me with his hip and my coffee spilled. 'Behave, wife. But no. One is enough.'

'Oh quick, the launch is coming into the bay. 'As we hurried down the hill, I scoffed my toast, and drained my coffee and then passed the empty mug to Rafe as I wiped my mouth, and brushed the crumbs off my shirt.

As we reached the steps at the bottom of the hill, Jiminy was tying off the rope.

I was surprised to see how many people were on the boat, and then exclaimed as I realised Sienna was stepping onto the wharf. 'Look, Sienna's home.'

Rafe followed me as I walked quickly along to meet her. My smile widened as I noticed the man behind her. 'And Danny's back!'

'Looks like I won the bet,' Rafe said as he

leaned down to brush his lips over my cheek.

'I didn't agree to a bet.'

'Piker,' he said, and then he stopped walking. 'Blimey, who's that guy?'

I followed his gaze to the boat and spotted the guy talking to Jiminy. He had to be one of the tallest men I had ever seen, and as Eliza had described, he was "built". Not to mention extremely good looking.

'That, my dear, is most probably our new lifeguard.'

I opened my arms to hug Sienna as she and Danny reached the end of the wharf. 'Well, don't you two look happy and relaxed,' I said.

Sienna's cheeks were pink, and she smiled at me and then up at Danny. 'We are.'

Epilogue
Tess

The first staff Christmas party on Pentecost Island was in full swing. Tess had finished up at the office, insisting that Nell knock off first to go and get ready for the party. Nell had finished the check ins while Tess ran the reports in the back office.

Once she'd finished, she checked that the guests on the veranda were being looked after by the casual restaurant staff over from Hamo. Jiminy was coming back at midnight to take them back across the Passage, with the staff who'd come over for the function.

Tess hurried to her room, had a quick wash, changed her clothes, and put on some lipstick. She hadn't eaten since lunchtime and the aroma of the curries the casual staff had put on made her stomach grumble. Pulling her door shut behind her, she made her way down the steps towards the restaurant. The music was loud and had a great beat, half a dozen couples were already on the dance floor, and as she walked along the path, she was sure it was Rafe she saw dip Pippa almost to the floor in a fancy move. Sienna and Danny were cheek to cheek dancing slowly, despite the disco beat. The tables were full of happy people speaking loudly to be heard over the music. Pippa had even brought the housemaids and kitchen hands over for the party.

It was going to be a great night and Tess was looking forward to letting her hair down for the first time in a couple of years. She loved working on Pentecost Island, and it had given her a chance to consider her options and what she was going to do with her life. Cherry had suggested her to Pippa, and when the job had turned into a traineeship, Tess had been ecstatic. Working on the island was the first step in a new career.

She hurried along the path and when she was almost to the bar, someone stepped from the rainforest and blocked her way.

'Tess,' an all too familiar voice said.

Her eyes widened and her hand went to her mouth. 'What the hell are you doing here?'

'I need you to keep a secret.'

***

What is the secret that Tess has to keep?

Book 9, Tess in the Pentecost Island series is available for pre-order in eBook here:

books2read.com/u/b5kEvA

and available in print from Annie's store:

https://www.annieseaton.net/store.html

Tess Andersen is well and truly over her family telling her what to do, criticising her career choices, and her boyfriends, but now she has found a happy niche on Pentecost Island. When her past catches up with her with the arrival of millionaire, Zac Montgomery, Tess has some choices to make. Zac has a reputation that precedes him wherever he goes—thanks to a former partner and social media. He knows he will have to work hard to overcome it now that he has found Tess, his first love, again. Can he convince Tess he's not the bad boy of his reputation?

Other Books

Whitsunday Dawn
Undara

Osprey Reef (2021)

Porter Sisters Series

Kakadu Sunset

Daintree

Diamond Sky

Hidden Valley (2021)

Pentecost Island Series (2020)

Pippa

Eliza

Nell

Tamsin

Evie

Cherry

Odessa

Sienna

Tess

Isla

Sunshine Coast Series

Waiting for Ana

The Trouble with Jack

Healing His Heart

Bondi Beach Love Series

Beach House

Beach Music

Beach Walk

Beach Dreams

The House on the Hill

Second Chance Bay Series

Her Outback Playboy

Her Outback Protector

Her Outback Haven

Her Outback Paradise

Love Across Time Series

Come Back to Me

Follow Me

Finding Home

The Threads that Bind

Others

The Trouble with Paradise

Deadly Secrets

Adventures in Time

Silver Valley Witch

The Emerald Necklace

Worth the Wait

Ten Days in Paradise

Her Christmas Star (2021)

About the Author

Finalist for the NZ KORU award 2018 and 2020.

Winner ...Best Established Author of the Year 2017 AUSROM

Long listed for the Sisters in Crime Davitt Awards 2016, 2017, 2018, 2019

Finalist in Book of the Year, Long Romance, RWA Ruby awards 2016

Winner ...Best Established Author of the Year 2015 AUSROM

Winner ...Author of the Year 2014 AUSROM

Best Established Author, Ausrom Readers' Choice 2017

Book of the Year (Whitsunday Dawn) Ausrom Readers' Choice Awards 2018

Annie lives in Australia, on the beautiful north coast of New South Wales. She sits in her writing chair and looks out over the tranquil Pacific Ocean. She has fulfilled her lifelong dream of becoming an author and is producing books at a prolific rate.

She writes contemporary romance and loves telling the stories that always have a happily Ever after. She lives with her very own hero of many years and they share their home with Toby, the naughtiest dog in the universe, and Barney, the rag doll kitten, who hides when the grandchildren come to visit.

Stay up to date with her latest releases at her website: http://www.annieseaton.net